DON'T TRY
THIS AT HOME

DON'T TRY THIS AT HOME

Angela Readman

LONDON · NEW YORK

First published in 2015 by And Other Stories
London – New York
www.andotherstories.org

'Don't Try This at Home' was shortlisted for the Costa Short Story
Award 2012. 'Conceptual' first appeared in *Burner* magazine (2012).
'There's a Woman Works Down the Chip Shop' was first published
in the *Root* anthology (Iron Press, 2013). 'Birds Without Wings' first
appeared in the Asham Award winners' anthology, *Once Upon a Time
There Was a Traveller* (Virago, 2013). 'Dog Years' first appeared in *Gigantic
Sequins* (2013). 'The Keeper of the Jackalopes' won the Costa Short Story
Award 2013 and was first published by the *Guardian* online in 2014.

ISBN 9781908276520
eBook ISBN 9781908276537

A catalogue record for this book is available from the British Library.

CONTENTS

DON'T TRY
THIS AT HOME

DON'T TRY THIS AT HOME

I cut my boyfriend in half; it was what we both wanted. I said we could double our time together. He said he could be twice as productive. I don't think it would have worked with just anyone at any time. It had to be now.

Daniel got a spade off his mother that had belonged to his father, and to his father – both men who were never really all there. He lay on the bench in the concrete back garden, knees bent to squeeze in. The yard was carpeted with silver slug trails. I suppose we could have used the kitchen floor, but I didn't want to scratch the tiles.

'Are you sure?' I said.

'Yup.'

I stood over Daniel with a spade in my hand. He didn't look at me. He looked up, waiting to see the sky divide. I thought about saying 'I love you' or something in case it all went wrong, but I didn't want to admit it crossed my mind.

'One, two . . . ' I brought the spade down on three with my eyes shut. There was a second when I wanted to stop, but mid-air the spade hurtled towards my original intention, with or without all of me on board. The metal sliced through bone, chimed on the concrete like a bell. I opened my eyes. My boyfriend was staring at me with the spade in my hand. And my boyfriend lay looking up at the sky. He turned to look at himself, sitting at the opposite end of the bench.

'How do you feel?' I asked.

'Fine.'

'Weird, fine.'

He stood up and put his arms round me. And he just sat there watching himself. Both Daniels looked exactly the same, though the one hugging me had slightly rounded shoulders, a bit of a stoop. He wrapped me in his arms as if reminding himself how, rubbing his fingers up and down my back to remember how it felt.

Neither the huggy boyfriend nor the one on the bench asked me how I felt about the whole thing. It's ok; I suppose some things just seem so much bigger for one person than another. But I sort of wished he had asked me what it was like, cutting him in half. I couldn't explain it. It reminded me of when I was five and watching a worm I spliced wriggle away from itself. I remember there was a twang of guilt when I saw the damp patch on the spade, yet I felt a bit like God.

*

I sliced my fiancé into quarters; it seemed the thing to do. We didn't do it right away. After the first time we went out to celebrate. The bartender glanced at my boyfriend with his arm around me. Then he looked at the other him, eyeing up the slot machine; I wondered if he thought I was going out with twins. Daniel's phone beeped, he texted, and sat holding my hand, looking at me as if we'd just met and I was all interesting, unpredictable, again. It cost more to buy drinks than usual, but it didn't matter at the time.

'Have a nice day,' I said.

'Yeah,' he said.

Daniel lay in bed beside me and watched himself leave for work. There was no conflict. I imagined he'd argue with himself to decide which part of him got to stay home with me, but it didn't happen that way. On weekdays the split came in handy. I wasn't working. All day I did housework, sent out CVs, painted rooms and alphabetised books to show him I was earning my keep. Sometimes I made love with the Daniel that stayed home. It was better than it had been in a while. Afterwards, he helped me paint the kitchen. He yawned when he got back from the office, eating meatballs with printer ink on his fingers. And he stretched where his back ached from reaching the ceiling, white paint in his hair. The white streaks sort of suited him, I could almost imagine him when he was old.

Once, I asked Daniel about how he proposed. Was he nervous? Scared?

Part of him was, he said. The other didn't know he was going to do it till the words popped out of his mouth. He was joining the lottery syndicate at work, and he was smearing the glass counters of jewellery shops. He stared at rows of engagement rings, trying to interpret what each one said.

'I'm tired,' he said.

'I've booked a table for us at Vincenzo's,' he said, putting on a clean shirt.

'Do you mind if I just stay in and crash?'

Daniel ordered the house white, putting his hand in his pocket every few minutes to check everything was where it should be. And he twirled in his desk chair in front of the computer, yawning and clicking links just to see what they were. I don't know exactly what he was looking at when he looked into my eyes and went down on one knee.

It was the wedding, I think, that made us do it again. Things to save for, dreams to buy. We went to buy paint for the hall during the week and carried ladders home on the bus.

'We could do with another car,' I said.

He sighed. He sighed, from both sides of the room like a draft blowing through a slightly open door.

'I could get a job,' he said. Standing straight, his stoop was hardly noticeable. He looked like he was manning up to the idea.

'You don't have to,' I said.

I covered the bridal magazines with my elbows. I didn't want a big do, not really. Common sense told me it was mad, but a bit of me couldn't imagine missing out on the opportunity for people to congratulate me for the first time in my life. What if it was the last?

They took Daniel's 'brother' on at the engineering firm where he already worked. The night before he started he laid his clothes on the chair like a kid before a new term at school. When he'd been working for a while, I asked him, 'Do you have lunch with yourself? I mean, at work?'

'No,' he said.

'Why not?'

'I'm my superior, it's not done.'

When he got home from work again – later because he walked home while his superior took the car – I asked, 'Why don't you have lunch with yourself at work?'

'We don't have anything to talk about,' he said.

'What do you mean?' I said.

'I don't know. Forget I said anything.'

He was too tired to talk. It was easier not to. Lately, when he came home he talked about work, and he also talked about work. He didn't notice my new spaghetti recipe, and was too wired to have an early night. I missed him. Our bank balance was fatter, but our evenings were so skinny I could see bone. The solution was clear.

I stood with the spade in the yard, tarp on the ground. Daniel lay down, ready as he'd ever be.

'Shall I just do half of you?' I asked. He turned his head to one side and looked himself in the eye.

'It wouldn't be right somehow,' he said.

'It wouldn't be fair on part of me or something,' he said.

'How would we know which bit of me to split?'

I'd no idea. In the interests of symmetry, I brought the spade down. I aimed for the waist both times, but on the second strike the spade hit at an angle in the middle of his belly button. Daniel noticed a crisp packet that had strayed into the yard and got up to get it. He looked at his phone. He said he fancied a beer. And, again, he hugged me tight like someone trying to get that little bit more out of a tube of toothpaste, squeeze out that little extra bit of love. I noticed one of the new Daniels was a teensy bit shorter than before. He was listing to one side, one leg was longer than the other. I tilted, looking over his shoulder at the rest of him, barely noticing himself in my arms.

I diced my husband into pieces eventually. I never thought it would come to that; he was always too much. Daniel stood at the altar, and he . . . I'm not sure what else he did, I didn't ask. It made sense not to have all of him there. Our big day was bigger than us. What if that childish bit of him that still sniggered at words like 'moist' or 'flange' slipped out in front of my mum? That bit of him, and me, that would rather have worn cowboy hats in a five-minute ceremony during Happy Hour in Las Vegas had no place here.

'If any of you know cause, or just impediment, why these two persons should not be joined together in holy matrimony, may you speak now or forever hold your peace.'

I heard Daniel shuffle at the back of the church, and I closed my eyes to be kissed. We stood outside for pictures on the grass, ducking here and there to avoid including the gravestones. I saw him out of the corner of my eye, leaning against the church wall wearing jeans. In some of the photos he was there in the background in a T-shirt, stubble on his chin, just watching himself stand next to my father in a suit like it was on TV. I axed the photos from the album; I didn't ask where the other parts of him had been.

It was a few years till we got the spade out again. It was Daniel's idea. He could work more, pay my loan off, since it was clear no one was hiring philosophers. He lined himself up against the garage wall. I swiped the spade through him like a credit card.

My husband worked in engineering, and he worked as a draughtsman at his firm. He drove a taxi, and he drove lorries of toilet rolls to Wales. He worked in a place that sold scuba gear, and he did the odd night on the door in swanky bars in town. He lived at the gym, and only lifted the remote. Some colleagues called him Daniel, some Dan, Danny, Danny Boy, one of the guys at the gym called him The D-man for no reason I could understand. I never knew how much of him would be home any night because of his hours. It was hard to keep track. The important thing was we got by, and he was with me, mostly.

'Do you still love me?' I said.

Daniel looked around as if waiting for someone to walk through the door and answer for him. 'Of course, I do,' he said.

*

On our wedding anniversary I called a meeting, a sort of regrouping I suppose. I steamed mussels, baked bread and bought wine. Most of my husband came. He was away making a delivery, and he was at the bar, but the rest of him was home. We sat around the kitchen table. I looked at him and saw him – tall, toned and tanned, and I saw his belly, his slight stoop, his total focus and his distraction. He was unable to take anything seriously and was totally annoyed by everything on the news. He looked at himself watering down his wine, and cracked open a beer.

'My job isn't me,' he said, rubbing his belly.

I think he meant driving a taxi, but I wasn't sure. Parts of him were dead ringers for others, but some were so different they were like what twins would be if one grew up in a burger joint and the other on a farm. Daniel opened crisps and watched himself not listen. He didn't say another word. Later, in bed, I nestled into him, trying to make something better, but I wasn't really sure if I had the right part of him in my arms.

I discovered my husband was cheating a few weeks before Christmas. We were shopping near the market, Daniel carrying the bags. And I saw him grab the hand of a frizzy blonde woman with a dog in her handbag, not far from the bar where he worked. Daniel stared at himself ducking into a doorway, hands all over the woman, unruly, urgent, kissing like he was fourteen and would explode if he didn't. I made my way through the crowds. I lost them between buggies and indecisive shoppers sampling chutneys at the farmers' stall. I stood looking around, shoppers everywhere, door after door. Daniel stared at the empty doorway where part of him had dragged the woman for kisses that wouldn't wait. He stood still on the street. It was hard to pull him away.

'How could you do that?' I said. 'Why?'

'I wish I knew,' he said.

I wasn't enough for my husband. I realised it shortly after our sixth married Christmas. I cooked turkey. Daniel ate the drumstick, and wanted only the lean meat. He opened a can of beer at lunchtime, watched TV, and had the odd sip of wine while helping me peel the sprouts. We sat at the table. Something was missing. Part of him was driving a taxi all over town.

'Think of the money. Most of me will be there,' he had said, running his hand over his bristly shaved head.

I wanted to protest, but I didn't. I didn't want to think about what was missing. He was here, crashed out in front of the Queen's Speech, and helping me do the dishes. He gave me a gold necklace and kissed me next to the tree, then went to the bathroom to text the woman with the dog in her bag. He gave me underwear that didn't fit, and he found me an antique desk. He bought a new TV instead of doing presents, and he wrapped up a new roasting tray, a bar of chocolate and socks. It was a typical Christmas, but I kept thinking of him in his taxi. When he came home at about two and crashed, I slipped out of the crowded king-sized bed and sifted through the pockets of his jeans on the bathroom floor. There was no money in them, tips in clear bags awaiting the bank, just his phone. I opened it like a book I didn't really want to read. I stared at photos of a chubby woman in a ponytail. She was wearing pink sweat pants and a paper hat, holding up a baby dressed like a reindeer. There were photos of the reindeer baby and another child, a boy of maybe three or four, grinning, holding a big yellow cab in a box up to the camera. I looked closely at the cluttered room with a cheap carpet, the same clock on the mantelpiece that we gave to the charity shop last year. I put the phone down. Part of Daniel had a whole other family, part of him didn't want kids. He'd say that fireplace behind the reindeer baby was tacky. Everything about the room was so ordinary; he hoped for more. He liked everything clean. He wanted to do something extraordinary in life, to be going somewhere, but sometimes tacky and ordinary were enough.

I went out to the yard and picked up the spade, wanting to slice myself in two, but I didn't think it would work. I was always here, completely. I couldn't imagine being anywhere else. I took the spade up the stairs and stood by the bed, watching Daniel sleep, the hair he'd grown into a ponytail again spread on the pillow, wax from his business-savvy haircut on the pillowcase next to it, his shaved head nestling into the sheets. I nudged the taxi-driving bit of him with the edge of the spade. It sliced through, a knife through the butter of his belly, though I barely touched him. He woke suddenly, four eyes opened wide. The rest stayed asleep.

'I found the photos,' I said. 'Aren't you happy with me?'

He looked at himself snoring. Then he looked back at me.

'Most of me is; then there's that little bit that thinks: what would my life be like with someone else? Who would I be?'

He got out of bed. He got out of bed. Both halves stood, packed one case between them and left without looking back at himself.

I'm still married. I have a husband with a little pot belly, a stoop to his shoulders and a funny belly button. He never leaves my side. Sometimes, other parts of Daniel come home, a slightly taller guy with flowers who looks, to me, no different than he did the day we met, though he is older, squishier and tougher-skinned. The rest of him is elsewhere, living in a quayside apartment with a woman with a dog with a fancy haircut, or working around the clock to make ends meet and put food on the table for three kids. He is rich, and he is poor. He is tired, and loves skiing in Italy. He is ambitious, and has given in. We are happy, and bored. Sometimes I miss him. I see him look out of the window, wondering where part of him went. I stand beside him, handing him tea. And I wonder if someone somewhere is doing the same, looking out of windows, longing for the part of him that's with me.

CONCEPTUAL

We lived as conceptual artists. It's what we were. If anyone wanted to know who we were, they had only to look. On special occasions, my family cut their clothes from paintings. Mum wore Botticelli. My sister wore Ophelia's drowning dress, and Dad was the king some woman in a medieval painting swept around. I wore a smock from a haystack. Kids called me Yoko Weirdo.

My mother invited the kids to my birthday party. She shook hands with other parents from behind a canvas. We cut cake to throw at billboards. I blew out a candle and wished we could have normal parties. I wanted to wear Nike or Topshop like everyone else. But when the guests left and it was just us, we were happy. Never bored, we spent winter evenings catching the moon in a bucket a hundred times.

School was something else. The teacher gave my art homework an F. My canvas was blank with a small hole in the centre. I brought it home and Mum hung it over the window. We sat in front of it like a TV, watching the sun make the white yellow then pink, then a star fit through the hole. Mum said it was the best painting she'd ever seen. She attached the hair from my brush to her wall and added the tally of my sister's freckles to the chart. Every summer vacation speckled on my sister's face was counted like commemorative coins of hot days.

Sometimes we got notices from the Residents' Association about the canvas in the yard with the leftovers of our meals on. Kids pushed me in the dirt and told me to count every grain. I'd go home angry, ready to lecture my family on the advantages of being boring. But there was my sister carrying a bag of peas under her arm, leaving one wherever she went. From the window I saw little green dots everywhere. Birds spread their wings everywhere she'd been. There was too much to see to stay angry. I looked at a cloud and asked it to gather vapours of how I felt.

Then things changed. Mum gave Dad a Valentine's of skin she had shed in the past year. He flew a photo of her up to the sky and let go of the strings. There was nothing conceptual about the woman he left us for. She owned a paper shop. It was nowhere near as exciting as it sounds. It wasn't a shop built of paper which the wind moved to where it was needed. It just sold stationery and magazines. Dad used to go in there with a scalpel, cutting ads out of magazines to replace them with instructions for origami butterflies. He was always an artist, but his talent was a sad burden. His biggest project had never been realised. He had dreamed of living in a house that was a giant sledge. When the city denied his building application he had started to send all his mail with pictures of his face on instead of a stamp. Black ink had etched his brow with worry lines. Only this could show him how he really felt. When that wasn't enough, he gave up the life and moved on to the new project of living with the most ordinary woman in the world.

Art continued without him; it was all we knew. Mum was an idea machine, picking up the slack for them both. In his absence, she made a list of everything that needed to be done in the house, then went to bed, as if writing it down would make every chore do itself while she slept. The next stage of the project was to stay in bed until we came looking. When she got up she hung the sheets from the bed round the room like a tent, still unwashed. She looked out at the tree Dad had planted and wept tiny stones. Next, she started working on learning how she really smelled. She didn't wash or change her clothes. Her skin was a project growing each day like thin tissue. Art was everywhere all the time.

Mum took a photo of the woman in the paper shop and made it into a canvas. We threw cookies at it before bed. Then, she reprinted the photo, cut it into sections and sent pieces of it to everyone she knew. The paper-shop woman received her own mouth in the post. The police came to our house. The word 'harassment' punched Mum in the chest. She tried to explain how she just wanted to give people something to carry with them all day, show them parts of themselves they didn't understand. The police looked around the house and saw the canvas of Dad's mistress covered in chocolate and crumbs. Child Protection came and typed reports about the dirty sheets and the peas all over the floor. They promised to return.

Mum had to stop her art until my sister and I were eighteen, or we'd be placed in a less artistic home. Our neighbours threw stuff over the fence. Someone sprayed 'LEAVE' on our canvas of Western waste.

'Why won't they leave us alone?' Mum said.

She wished she could make her body a canvas clothed only by whatever people passing her drew on it, but she loved us too much to try. She cleaned the house and cut her hair. Piece by piece, my sister and I carried Mum's art to the basement. Mum couldn't show anyone how she felt without it. She bought a tracksuit and wore it. Me and my sister got winter coats.

It was only then I understood what any of our art had ever done. My mother dropped me at school like everyone else, dressed in nylon, a sandwich in my bag instead of a slice of the moon. And all I could think about was finding a stone, the same size and shape as me, ground down into fine powder. I wanted to give it to everyone every time I was called to crack a smile I didn't mean.

SURVIVING SAINTHOOD

You dip a toe into the swimming pool, a forgotten plastic dolphin bobs up and down. Mom is wearing that turquoise costume, pulling Lycra out of her butt crack. Everything will change. You don't know this; I do the knowing for us both.

Mom turns towards a wolf-whistle the man on a sun lounger is too old to give and she's too wobbly to receive. The man has a beer. It's 6.35. She looks over, deciding if he's crazy, wasted or just bored. There's no one else around so she takes those off-season baby steps towards him. Your water wings flap in the air, want to fly.

'Can I go in?' You stamp a splashy foot, stick out a ruffled behind.

'Not yet,' Mom yells, turning back to the man. He is all smiles, between sips.

You don't know what it's like to want to close your eyes so bad. Mom's looking at the plump man as if he's a life raft we can all climb aboard and drift into the sunset on. Under my sunglasses, I blink. I won't see her fall in

love again. She always drowns. Sssshhh. Mom's breath is
a leak. Your water wings are slowly losing air.

'Lose the wings,' I say.

The cap on the left wing isn't all the way in. I blow
with my back to the pool, all eyes on Mom. Her hope fits
like hot pants she's not young enough to wear.

The man points, legs of his chair scrape concrete as
he rushes to his feet. Shouts. And Mom's running, hands
automatically fly to her chest, clutch her jiggles to prevent
herself spilling out of her costume. She dives into the pool
and rises with you in her arms.

'Won't someone help?' she yells, laying you on the deck.

The man bounces into the motel. And Mom keeps
breathing, pinching your nose, blowing into your mouth.
Where did she learn CPR? Your body rises and falls, inflatable, doll-like. And like anyone with a doll, I'm staring at it,
wishing it to come to life. I slide my sunglasses onto my skull
and stand still. You don't know what it's like to do nothing,
to know that, whatever happens, nothing is your default
setting. It's realised in seconds, one moment that rolls like
live coverage for a lifetime. I'll be tying my shoelaces, or
telling someone the capital of Peru, and stuff splashes up.

I see you, that plastic dolphin, Mom's 'Won't someone
help?' One water wing sighs in my hand. I stand by the
pool. I never dive.

*

This is the moment life can drift into past tense. It happened so fast. We *saw* the doctor, we *asked* another specialist, you *went* for another scan. There are moments to really be somewhere, and hours to barely be there. Everything was different. It hadn't soaked in yet. Mom's eyes lurched to the door at the squawk of the nurse's rubber shoes. There were strawberries printed on her clothes. You'd have asked why the nurses all wore pyjamas – if it was to make the patients feel less left out. She hooked up a tube to suck saliva from your mouth. If her bright clothes could talk they'd be singing: *Don't worry, you aren't in hospital. This is one big pyjama party! Here, have Jell-O, a fruit cup.* No, not you. Your eyes were shut. I sat on a plastic chair. Mom gripped my hand. 'Everything will be ok.'

The doctor's stethoscope looked too cold for you. Everything always was. On days when the breezeway's plastic roof crackled in the sun like bacon you used to kick your legs and moan, 'Cold.'

'I think she's got the words wrong,' Mom said. 'She says cold when she's hot, and hot when she's cold.'

You never said how things were. You only said how you wanted things to be. Then, you said nothing. You got fed through a tube in your stomach. I got addicted to soup from the vending machine, sticking my finger into Dixie cups, slurping up salty goop that wouldn't dissolve.

'Where there's life . . . ' Mom said.

There's waiting, waiting for someone to wake up.

'It's unusual: all her vitals are good,' the specialist said. 'Kidneys, heart, lungs . . . '

He didn't have to mention your brain. If he was kind of cute, Mom didn't mention it. Once, when I had tonsillitis, a different doctor flattened my tongue with a wooden paddle and said, 'He has your eyes.' Mom assessed a white band of skin on his finger that had never seen daylight and turned up her laugh like the brightness on a TV. We returned four times.

That was the old Mom. You wouldn't recognise this one, pure Mom mode. The Mega Mom. She sang about cats in cradles and promised you the moon.

Your body rises and falls, inflatable, a doll. And like anyone with a doll, I stare at it wishing it would come to life.

You came home on a Thursday. The men scraped the paint on the doorframe carrying you in. The scratch is still there in the woodwork, like a cut that won't scab. The doctor recommended a facility with 24/7 care. Mom shook her head. She could do it. You should be at home. She looked at catalogues with bedpans in and measured my room.

I didn't complain, honest, not that much. You needed the space, the bed with sides like a cage, diaper storage, the oxygen tank, just in case. Every time I opened my mouth to speak about school, ask what was for dinner, or complain about my sneakers being too tight, I sounded small, my voice scrunched into a whine.

'Not everything's about you,' Mom said. 'Think of your sister. Don't you know how lucky you are?'

I did. I lay in my room listening to the drone of your electric bed and the buzz of Mom brushing your teeth. Then it stopped. It must be 9pm. Mom was Nursemom. Shark-like, if she stopped moving she'd die. She rolled you over, checked for sores and switched on your TV to colour in the silence. I flicked on my TV to see what she was thinking. It was some show about miracles.

I counted the cowgirls on the wallpaper in your old room. Mom had a new hobby: screaming at airlines. You were a fire hazard. You could block the aisles. Then, she was packing your case. The airline bumped you up to first for nothing more than an article in the paper. 'I am taking my daughter to a monastery in Europe where the sick have been cured. It has been a difficult year, since the accident,' Mom said. 'I can't tell you what this means to us. The airline has been amazing.'

I was whisked off to the grandparents. Every day at 11am Gran said, 'Starbucks time!', slopped milk, sugar and instant coffee into a pan and boiled it to the bubble.

'I wonder if your mother and Jessica are having a nice time,' she said. 'I wish they'd phone.'

We slurped sweet milky coffee opposite a photo of a little me and baby you on the wall. I looked like someone had placed an anvil in my lap and said 'cheese'.

Only you know what the Virgin Mary thought about it all, maybe. Mom buzzed louder than a moth skirting the zapper. The vacation was amazing, she said. You rolled to the front of the queue at the convent like VIPs at Disneyland. Inside, a monk whispered in your ear.

'What did he say?' I asked, foiling a Toblerone.

Mom disassembled the praying mantis of her hands. Thumbs up.

'I don't know,' she said. 'He wasn't speaking American, or French.'

You won't remember how badly she wanted to look clever the year Dad left. She kept dropping French phrases at dinner, *ah fromage, jambon*. She plonked lettuce on the table, announcing *salaud* with all the glee of a schoolgirl spelling matricide or patricide.

'Your sister received a message from the Virgin Mary, the monk whispered it to her,' Mom said. 'Something happened: she moved. It's a miracle.'

'How?'

'She twitched.'

'How do you know it was the Virgin Mary? How do you know, for sure?'

'I don't,' Mom said. 'I choose to believe it. I don't need to know everything. The message was for your sister, not me. Doesn't she look different? See that? She's smiling. Doesn't she look like she's smiling?'

I looked for the miracle pasted all over you. You lay on your pillow, breathing, a nylon sunflower clipped to your hair, lips shiny as wax fruit.

The smiling plastic dolphin bobs in the pool.

A Miracle Girl is never alone. Mom cashed in a pension and hired a retired nurse called Isola to come in five days a week. Isola was a small woman with hair like scuzzy foamed milk. Occasionally, she spoke about her son who died in the marines, but mostly she said stuff like, 'God has a purpose for everyone' and 'Where there's life, there's . . . ' Pictures of the Virgin Mary in the kitchen, your bedroom, the john. They popped up like the cut-out paper Barbies you used to leave everywhere you went: Barbie at the discount store; Barbie caged with the rabbit Mom wouldn't buy at the pet store; Barbie soaked, curling by the tub.

Mom was Bloggermom, a counter of blessings. It's rude to keep a miracle to yourself. She posted pictures of you and typed stuff like 'faith' and 'just knowing'. She *knew* you were special now, she could *feel* it, she said. The comments and letters took her by surprise. People believed in you, I don't know if you know that, if you felt you had 'followers', thousands of 'friends'. I got sick of never being able to get on the PC.

Every night, Mom slipped photographs of sick kids under your pillow and read you letters from strangers like bedtime stories.

'God bless you both. I know what you're going through . . . my son has ADD . . . my daughter has diabetes . . . my husband's battling with . . . You're in our prayers, Jessica. Please pray for us.'

I lay in my room listening, biting my fingernails to stumps. The cowgirls on the walls watched me lick blood from my hands.

I was watching a show about sleepwalking when Isola screamed in the kitchen. This lady psychologist on TV fiddled with her wedding ring and spoke about things people don't know they're doing. One of her patients got up every night to make sleepsandwiches, some guy played sleephoop, a kid in pyjamas walked to the top floor, opened the window and sleepstoodontheledge.

Isola gasped through the hallway, holding up glistening fingers: 'Our Lady is weeping for Jessica!'

Mom put down the hairbrush, left it on your chest like Buckaroo and ran.

We stared up at a slip of oil on the cheek of the Mary painting above the fridge.

'It's a miracle,' Mom said.

Isola was crying, so was Mom. I left the pair dabbing painted eyes with cotton wool, closed my door and hurled a compass out of my bedroom window.

Once, I stroked the painting. The tears smelt of pesto. The oily olive waft mingled with the rusty smell on my arms. Each night I catalogued any small wound the day dished out: papercuts on a finger, a puncture wound on a wrist, a bruise on a shin where I wheelied off my bike. I was obsessed with the slightest scrape: I had to know where I was when it happened, who was there, why, like I was investigating a crime. The shins spoke for themselves, but I couldn't account for the scabs on my arms. I came up with a theory I was a scratcher. I guess I scratched the same place in my sleep till I bled. I locked all my plastic superheroes, pencils and pens in my closet and dropped the key in the pot of paint that never got around to covering the cowgirls on the walls. If I was a sleepscratcher, anything with sharp edges could make things worse.

It was a year for signs and stealing, nothing major, anything I could get: dog chews from pet stores, handkerchiefs, Duck Tape, maxi pads. Mom photographed splotchy sores on your ankles and compared you to Jesus. Whatever. I changed into a black sweatshirt to go help empty the garage. The radio was fading out Johnny Cash.

'Man in Black!' Mom said, 'Don't you ever want to be colourful?'

'Don't you ever want to blend in more?'

She handed me a broom. Isola had the idea to convert the garage into a chapel for your visitors – all those Hallelujahs wouldn't fit in the house.

'You don't need this,' Mom said, holding a skateboard by a wheel.

'I do. I just don't use it.'

I scurried inside for the bathroom. On the way, I wandered into your room. Was it ever mine? The walls were oyster. Pearly cards and gifts squatted among medical supplies. I flicked open a card: 'God bless you, Jessica. They gave me six months. I wrote to you. Now I'm better . . . ' I put it down and slipped a glass angel on the nightstand into my pocket. You slept on, surrounded by angels, an army of paper, glass and plastic guardians.

You flap your water wings by the pool, want to fly.

On Monday, I slipped the angel into the backpack of a girl at school with a blind brother – sort of stealing in reverse. It felt so good I thought I'd never steal again.

'Grab something out the fridge, Ben. I haven't time,' Mom yelled on Tuesday.

It was another frantic morning. You had a cold. The doctor was coming. I raided another lunchbox from a locker with a 007 combination. Sandwiches shaped by heart-shaped cookie cutters, crusty brownies, optimistic apples slipped in by healthy Moms: I ate the lot, licked bloody mayo off my fingers and stuffed the napkins up my sleeve.

You didn't have to remember stuff like birthdays. You hit eleven, but you were still always five, swaddled in pink T-shirts covered in kittens, Sesame Street duvets on your bed. I was sixteen. Isola burnt a Betty Crocker. Mom opened a medical bill and promised we'd celebrate properly next month. The cards slumped on the kitchen counter, fenced in by your letters. I gave myself the gift of fingering a girl.

We were ditching. I ditched gym eight out of ten and I always cut French. (Who needed to know what Mom said that summer?) The girl sat on the floor of the storage room behind the canteen. Everything smelt of congealed pizza and the deodorant I caught her stuffing up a sleeve and squirting at her armpits.

'I thought I was the only one who knew about this place?' I said.

She shrugged. 'No one's the only person who knows anything.'

I sat beside her, surrounded by vast bottles of ketchup and monster cans with terse labels. I was waiting for the bell. So was she. I put a hand on her knee. She didn't move. I took it as a sign.

I withdrew my fingers, aware, so aware, of my sleeves sliding down my wrists. If she didn't want me to stop, she didn't say.

'Do you think I'm pretty?' she asked. 'Amy Morgan called me a pig yesterday.'

I saw her look at me, waiting for me to say yes, knowing it was some sort of fingerer's etiquette. I looked away, unable to say a word. The question depressed me to death.

I slide my sunglasses onto my skull. I stand by the pool. I never dive.

'Hey, what's wrong with you? You're bleeding.' She reached for a blood-streaked hand. I clamped down my sleeves and ran.

Mom rubbed lotion into your hands. Your big day was approaching. The anniversary of 'your calling' was on Friday. People were coming from all over the country to pray all over you. I stole a box of tissues from by your bed. Let them sniff. I was out of there, on a bus across town.

The house had a swing set and a birdbath draped with Big Bird. I stood across the street and watched Dad push small twin boys on the swings. One looked like the good twin. One looked like the one who'd grow up and never get laid, even though he and his brother were supposed to be the same. Dad pushed one swing, then the other. The kids flew away, then came back. One, then the other.

You wouldn't know Dad looked different. You were barely here when he left. Once, Mom told me it was his idea to call you Jessica. Jess, Jessie, Jessie James. I guess he wanted to be clever, and Mom was stupid enough to let him. You stopped being an outlaw when you got miraculous on us. Everyone lengthened your name as if they just wanted it in their mouths a little longer. The only person who still called you Jessie was me.

The paralegal wife slipped outside with sunscreen. I sloped off to the dime store, killing time, pocketing a flag and a packet of Band-Aids. The swings were still when I returned. The kitchen window was misted with steam. I laid the flag on the porch, took a shit on it and ran. The whole bus ride home I regretted it. It would have been better to shit first and put the flag on top like an umbrella in a bad cocktail to make some sort of statement. I stated shit.

On Friday, I rolled my bike down the drive after school. The lawn swayed with strangers fanning themselves with bibles in the sun. The garage door was open. People on folding chairs prayed to oil stains on concrete. Others queued by the house, admitted by Isola to see you in pairs.

'You can pray with Jessica and ask her to pray for you,' she said. 'She always listens, she's non-verbal, but if you hold her hand it may move.'

I weaved through the crowd to the door, and was detained by some guy in a bandana. He rolled up his shirtsleeves to wave you in my face.

'Have you been before, dude? I visited last year. That little girl saved my life,' he said.

I looked at you in inky blue on his forearm, your name tattooed to his skin, bearded in hairs: *Saint Jessica*. I don't know what you cured him of, but it wasn't of being an asshole.

'Her name is Jessie,' I said. 'Jessie James, like the train robber.'

I pushed into the house and made for my room. Your bedroom door was ajar. I watched a young man and woman place a floppy baby on your bed and grip your hand. I recalled you asleep in theme parks, dropping off right there on a ride as if your fun circuit was fried. You'd be carried home, stiffening your legs against Mom's manoeuvring you into pyjamas, you'd mumble, 'Sleep. Sleep. Now.' I wondered if lying there was like that, if you just wanted to sleep and people kept keeping you awake by speaking your name, if it was like drifting off with the TV on and hearing it in your dreams.

'Do you want to pray with us?' the woman asked. She looked up, eyes like holy water. The baby gurgled on your bed.

I stand by the pool. I never dive.

I locked my door and sat on the bed. The cowgirls on the walls watched me wind bandages off my wrists, the punctures between the bones slowly weeping. Don't ask how often it has happened, I don't count. Don't ask why, I don't know. You'd call it a miracle, perhaps. I call it a pain, taping tissues to my skin all day, long sleeves, lying 'I'm cold' in July. It's cutting gym, stealing psychology textbooks and kind of hating yourself like that cutter chick at school. Except, I'm not that chick, I don't think. I've never cut myself to see why I'm bleeding. Not that I know of. I'm a sleepscratcher, or some such shit.

The walls hummed with the crying in your room. I could hear Mom join the couple with a fistful of tissues and a 'let it all out'. I pictured myself walking in with crucified arms held high, blood steadily flowing from my wrists, dripping onto your My Little Pony rug.

'Look Mom! No razors.' Mom would clap her hands in joy. Isola would piss. 'It's a miracle! The boy's special!' she'd say. Everyone on the lawn would fall to their knees, if I gave them a reason. I walked to the window and stared at strangers praying outside, waiting to be let in, misty-eyed and wilting in the sun. I closed the curtains, sucking a wrist. You can keep the prayers, all that hope, please, it's all yours. Honestly, I wouldn't know what to do with it.

THERE'S A WOMAN WORKS
DOWN THE CHIP SHOP

My mother was like a Custard Cream, nothing special, an ordinary sort of nice enough. She was just there, like gravity. There was no need to think about her. She was Mam-shaped, bits of her flattened under a white overall with pearly buttons. Then, one summer, she became Elvis. She was yawning, frying chips, and worried if there'd be enough hot water for a bath when she got in, then BAM! She was Elvis, hips a gogo, rocking onto the balls of her feet with only the counter between her and lasses screaming and promising to love her for ever. Maybe she just thought, 'Sod it. I'd make as good an Elvis as anyone.' Who doesn't want to be Elvis now and then?

The funny thing is, I don't think my mother was *ever* an Elvis girl. The radiogram went on only on Sunday mornings. She dusted with the aid of Julie Andrews singing about a nun's favourite things. All her Beatles records were before 'Lucy in the Sky'. I sat on the carpet and flipped through my mother's singles, her name written in a tight scroll round the run-out groove. She must have gone places she might lose them, I suppose, but I couldn't see where. She left school, got a job at the dogs and married the bloke who set the rabbit running. *If* she was *ever* going to be Elvis, you'd think it would have been then – somewhere between school and the man who made a greyhound whip itself into the shape of a winner. No. For my mother, becoming Elvis took time. We never deliberately listened to the King, but we knew how to dance to him. Maybe that's what she needed, someone who *just knew* the words to her songs.

Everyone knew my mother, from the waist up. She was the woman in the chippy – a portion on the stingy side to spitters, overly generous to anyone who said 'Please' and 'Thank you' (never 'Ta'). She knew if her regulars were the mushy peas or beans sort. That was it. Then came that lass. The lass looked like someone who finally got into her mam's make-up box and went mad. Black stuff all over her eyelids like tyre-tracks, her gaze was like a crash victim's. Chips. A mist of salt. No vinegar. Red cola. She came in with a slobbery ginger bairn in a pram and a fistful of coins like a piggy bank spewed in her hand.

'You want scraps?'

Mam held the vinegar, snowed on the salt and turned to the fridge for pop.

'I like your bobble,' the lass said.

'Sorry?'

She said it again.

My mother's hair came home every night smelling of other people's suppers. It grew long and dark and looked like it was waiting for her to become a beatnik to make it feel at home. It was permanently scraped back with one of my bobbles. This one had white spots on red, like a dice. What are the chances anyone would notice something so small? Who cares? Mam looked sort of stunned. Who comments on a bobble? There was something sad or lovely about it, it was hard to tell. The lass lined up coins on the steel in order of size. Nice enough lass. Friendly. Why? My mother wrapped the chips and threw in a free sachet of ketchup to hide her embarrassment.

On Saturday she came in with a haircut short enough to stop her needing to hold anything back. I ran my fingers along the back of my mother's tapered head. It felt shy, soft as suede. No accessories needed. No comment required. She didn't do much with it, but every morning, without trying, the top of her hair rose in a quiff, a wave swallowing her ordinariness.

'What's with this hair?' she murmured. 'Got a mind of its own.'

She patted it down. It popped back up.

'You look like my woodwork teacher, thinks he's all that,' Brian said.

I noticed just how black my mother's hair really was. It was the sort of black that made me look at roads and crows and decide 'black' needed more names. Elvis was waiting to enter the building. I don't think she could have stopped it if she'd tried.

She couldn't stop the lass with the ginger kid fancying chips.

'Long day, rushed off your feet I bet? Not long now,' the lass said, looking at the clock.

Mam lowered the basket into hissing fat, pausing to look at the lass. Thin, eczema on her knuckles, inquisitive chin. Her mouth had a look about it like it wanted to smile, if the woman behind the counter said anything that let it. I don't suppose my mother was used to considering how long she'd been working or if her feet hurt. They just existed, in a perpetual state of half-ache. She fastened her eyes on the lass now and smiled. Unexpectedly, a curl softly tugged her top lip. It wasn't her usual smile. It was all Elvis, a smile that lets a second breathe. I noticed her Elvis mouth, how much she looked like him in the face. I'd never thought that if Elvis was a woman, and worked in a chippy, he'd be my mam. But I could hardly see my mother for Elvis now. Elvis jiggled the chips, hips ticktocking like an over-wound clock, all because someone asked how she was. It was like the difference between being Elvis and not being Elvis was as simple as someone *really* looking and wondering how you feel.

'You're my last customer,' Mam said, like it was special. When Elvis said it, it was.

Then, as if forgetting something, she added, 'Cute bag.'

The bag was a stringy thing full of holes. Impractical, my mother would have called it, if she'd noticed. But Elvis liked it. The lass wriggled fingers in and out of her bag's strings, little fish caught in a net. Elvis grinned.

'Have fun,' the lass said, hugging her chips.

The woman behind the counter watched her walk past the manager pulling down the shutters. She smiled, leaning back against the yellow glass windows over the lamps heating the pies. Elvis stretched like a cat in the sun. Have fun, she drawled. It was an order no one ever placed. Elvis tugged a pouty lip, considering what it meant.

Now, I don't know exactly how often the lass came in the chippy, or when Gina became her name. I only got scraps, bits after, and what I saw when I called in to tell on Brian or get change for Spangles. I do know there was nothing special about her, except how she talked. Gina made conversation like a gardener, planting a seed and waiting to see what might grow. None of us knew a woman like that. Women in Hinton's were snipers.

'How you keeping?' was a loaded gun, mouths cocked, aimed to shoot rounds. Mam turned her trolley around to avoid friendly fire.

What really did it was wiring. Gina came in the chippy with a lamp bigger than her. Mam's quiff stood to attention. Behind the counter, the bottom half of her body tilted in a different direction all on its own.

'Youboughtsomethingnicesugar?' she said.

Now, this wasn't her at all. My mother was all salt 'n' vinegar, the odd splash of ketchup, but the way she spoke now made the lass shiver like something velvet was being draped around her neck.

'Lamp for the living room, if I ever get the plug on,' Gina said.

The woman in the chippy would have sympathised, but it wasn't her job to do more. Elvis had other ideas. He offered to take care of business. Mam went to Gina's after work with a screwdriver in her pocket. She wired the lamp, somehow turning her Elvisness on full-time.

Everything was different. It was the summer of Elvis, and Mam having a friend she didn't give birth to. Gina lived on the estate where houses had gardens. We stopped sitting in our slice of yard where the wall blocked the sun. The ginger toddler, Simon, bounced up and down in the open back door. We sunbathed, the grown-ups pulling weeds and mowing wonky lines in the lawn. All the usual stuff, but somehow less boring. Elvis made it fun.

Carrying stuff out for the scrap-man, the adults lifted one side of a fridge apiece, then creased up laughing like it told a joke. I listened to Elvis's laugh. I thought it made my mother's old one sound like something running out of batteries, barely used. The sun blazed. She sweated and shone, her skin a gold suit. She watered the roses and turned the hose on Gina with a wink.

'Eeee! Pack it in! Eeee!'

Gina squealed, ducking and diving around the garden, soaked through. I sat on top of the coal bunker, the hot felt almost burning my legs. I watched the wifey next door put out rubbish and linger on tiptoe by the fence, grass making her slippers damp. She stood there for ages, unable to tear her eyes off Elvis.

'You making that sarnie or what?' her husband yelled through the back door.

The smile on her face twitched like a curtain. She went in.

Brian tossed stones up to the coal bunker. He'd never be an Elvis man. Later, when I asked, 'Do you remember that amazing summer Mam was Elvis?' he wouldn't talk about it. By then, our mother was gran-shaped, and he liked that just fine. I had to wonder about it by myself.

'Why do we have to come here?' Brian said, skimming a stone off my foot. 'What's Mam doing that dopey smile for all the time?'

I thought about this. I didn't think a smile had to be clever or dumb – it just was. I looked down at Elvis and Gina taking a break: two tatty towels lying side by side on the grass. They turned towards each other, talking so quietly only a bee flying over might hear. Brian's ears were red with listening. Brothers. He didn't like going to Gina's. He liked it even less when her boiler broke and she stayed at ours. Even when we went to Sandsend for the day he walked ahead on his own, cheeks red as a slapped bum.

Elvis took Gina's hand, to steady her walking across the dunes, then dropped it as if it burned. Someone was coming. An old man and woman stopped to let a ratty dog do its business. I turned back to see the woman from my nan's street. What was her name? Gwenny, maybe; everyone Nan knew was a Gwenny or something like it. Every morning the women crossed paths on the way to and from the newsagent's. I'd shuffle as they stood still to chat, flowery headscarves flapping like parrots in the wind.

'What's wrong?' Gina said.

She looked at my mother looking down at the sand. The old man shook his head. His wife was muttering something I wasn't sure I heard. I think it was, 'You should be ashamed.'

Not till they walked on and Gina set up a windbreaker fort on the beach did I see Elvis again. Somewhere along the path my mother had taken his place.

Then, she was gone again – buried. Elvis grinned at his body of sand, the mermaid tail covering his hips. I swear, no one could stop looking. This was Elvis, right here. Elvis – bursting out of his sand tail and picking up Gina to toss in the sea like she weighed less than my mother's shopping bags.

'Do you like Gina, honey?' Elvis asked, tucking me in, sleepy with sea.

'I wished we lived with her all the time,' I said.

Mam sighed like an Elvis who didn't want to be famous, an Elvis realising the guitar he clutched was too small.

The queue in the chip shop didn't move as fast as it used to. Sometimes lasses hovered at the counter, smiling at Elvis. They looked at the menu unable to decide what they wanted. An Elvis pelvis rocked to sizzling fat like music. He whirled chips into paper and span round, laying them down. Some women applauded and blushed, placing a hand over their mouths to stop their hearts leaping out. And some didn't. They folded their arms. Tutted. The lady who lived next to Gina twisted her ring as her husband tapped his fingers on his wallet.

'What the fuck's taking so long?' he said.

Elvis turned from the pie window, sauntered to the counter and leaned forward.

'That's no way to talk in the presence of a lady, sir,' he said, head bowed.

'Pardon?' the man said. He looked at old men queue-ing behind him, blokes back from the football, and his wife at his side.

'I'll talk how the fuck I like in front of her, she's my wife,' he said.

'Maybe you should apologise,' Elvis said.

The wife tugged her husband's arm. 'Leave it,' she said.

He shrugged her off, pushing her into a stagger. Elvis slowly shook his head, then WHAM! A fist landed on the man's jaw with a cowboy-loud crack. Kids smudged their noses on the window trying to get a look in, 'Fight, fight, fight, fight!' The man stumbled back, the queue scattered like sparrows.

'You'll be sorry,' he said, rubbing his jaw.

'I am sorry,' Elvis said. 'I'm sorry for your wife.'

Everyone talked about the fight for weeks. The woman in the fishy went mental and knocked a guy out for no reason, people said. No, that wasn't it – she gave him a black eye for pushing in. No one was sure, not even the manager, who was at his sister's wedding. There was nothing he could do. No one actually complained. Elvis apologised to everyone present. It was free chips, no, it was free fishcakes, cod, all round.

It wasn't the punch that changed things, I don't think. It was something quieter that wiped the Elvis off my mother's face. It was pension night. The Gwenny we saw at Sandsend popped in for supper after the bingo.

'What can I get you?' Elvis beamed.

The old woman's mouth was a zip, syllables caught in her teeth.

'*You* can't get me anything,' she said.

The queue shuffled and whispered. They looked at Elvis, then the woman, and whispered again.

The old woman glared. She didn't place her order, and she didn't budge.

'What can I do for you?' the manager said.

He smoothed his comb-over over and walked to the counter to dip her haddock in the batter himself.

I looked towards Elvis, coins for Pineappleade sweating in my hand. Elvis wasn't there, only my mother, filling the box of wooden forks, looking like someone booed offstage.

'You still hanging about with that lass? What's her face?' Nan said. Her lips were a line.

'No.'

Nan nodded, broke out her stash of Bullseyes and squirrelled them back in her bag.

'Hear her husband's back. Best thing. Shame you can't find a good solid man,' Nan said.

'You make blokes sound like tower blocks,' Mam replied.

She looked out the window as if imagining women

who lived behind the walls of good solid men – constantly moving the furniture, repainting the doors.

Elvis had left the building. There was no sign of him at home. Mam brought in tea and dropped the biscuit tin like a sinking Titanic. I looked at the Custard Cream in my hand, the special pattern like a scrolly invitation on old-fashioned notepaper, then I dunked it in my tea. Mam hunched over the newspaper, ads for people next to lost cats and dogs. She circled 'GSOH' with a pen. Stepping out of the house in heels, for the first time in my life, she was Bambi learning to walk on ice.

'Did you have a nice time?' I asked later.

She took two bags of crisps out her bag and tossed us one each.

Brian buried his face in *Commando*.

'It was ok.'

I licked prawn cocktail off my crisps.

'Is no one nice?'

'They are, but . . . there's just . . . no . . . no . . . chemistry,' she said, slumping onto the couch.

It didn't seem she was talking to me or Brian. It was more something she had to say to herself, like the way she figured out the crossword by saying words aloud and counting the letters on her hand. I listened, picturing men in test tubes. My mother's laugh was a scientist's; none of her experiments was a success. She put her heels in the box and wrapped fish suppers in ads for men who liked long walks. Elvis was AWOL.

I didn't see a trace of him until tatty-picking week the following year, when some woman started popping into the chip shop on her way home from work.

'You always put on just the right splash of vinegar,' she said.

She clutched a note, looking at my mother and leaning up to the counter with a grin. Sandals slipped off the back of her feet. Chips. Pineapple ring. Curry sauce.

'Quiet night, eh?' she said.

And there was Elvis again, for a heartbeat, as if he'd never left and was just waiting in the wings – if my mother would allow him to make a comeback. Elvis looked at the lass. Feathery hair, pianist fingers laid flat on the counter, no ring, dimples between her eyes and lips. The woman in the chippy shrugged off a smile and stormed on the salt.

'You want scraps?' she said.

BIRDS WITHOUT WINGS

Last summer, it was me and Eva against everything evil in the world: swimsuits, kale, something that buzzed in our room. Yet I couldn't stop thinking about Diana Pinter, some girl at school who went to Paris with her mother. I lay on a bunk scratching mosquito bites and pictured them outside the Eiffel Tower, eating salad in the rain. I flicked through the magazines Mom posted, girls with eyes lost as gazelles. Their hair was molasses, candy-apple shiny, the colour of Twinkies. My stomach growled. It would be dinner soon, something steamed. A postcard and cash fell out of *Vogue*, Mom's handwriting like spun silk. *Hope you're having a good time. Be good! We'll go shopping when you get home.* I knew what 'be good' meant. I shoved the twenty in my sock and dangled to high-five Eva on the bottom bunk.

This summer would be different. Mom wanted us to take a trip. Dad was working and my brother wouldn't come. Ed was oddly self-sufficient. He lived in a fort of science books in his room: at nine, he wasn't interested in sports camp. If there'd been an accountancy camp he'd have jumped in line. A camp where boys learned to give bad financial news and crinkle their brows exactly like their fathers would suit him just fine.

'What do you think? Just the two of us,' Mom said. 'Won't it be fun?'

I wasn't sure. *Fun* and *Mom* went together as well as she said my shoes matched my blouse. I watched her fiddle with lilies in the vase in the lounge again, fingertips unable to resist trying to improve their elegance.

No camp! I thought. No hikes, kale or treasure hunts (hikes in disguise – except with fruit and a whittled wooden otter, rabbit, any animal that could be described as a 'critter', at the end).

'Where do you wanna go?' I said.

'Mexico,' Mom replied.

Not Paris or Venice, which was weird. Her friends usually took their daughters to glistening cities of tiny espresso cups and art galleries, to cram in a few more 'sit up straights' before school pushed them out into the world.

'Why Mexico?' I asked.

She let the lilies be, looking down like she did when she told Dad the drapes were a steal.

'I don't know. It's different,' she said. 'I read something about the spiritual side.'

I supposed being different was the appeal, and maybe the cost, though she'd never admit it. In the contest of who had the best holiday, I guessed spiritual trumped cultural every time.

'Suppose it might be cool,' I said.

Mom smiled, something up her cashmere sleeve. Mexico? Whatever. It couldn't do any harm. I phoned Eva to break the news.

'Mexico?' she said. 'Well, at least she won't make you go clothes shopping.'

She was wrong.

I followed my mother past counters like ice cubes. The air-con was on overdrive. My shirt stuck, sweat from the street chilled on my arms – shopping was a fever, hot and cold at the same time. My mother strolled, confident her hands were clean enough to stroke every dress on the rail. I pictured Diana Pinter and her mother swapping clothes in Parisian changing rooms, laughing when a cocktail dress suited Diana, and a pleated skirt and blazer looked inexplicably apt on her mom.

'How can I help?'

The assistant's suit was endive pale. She smiled at her commission in the form of a woman with a Chanel purse and hair like a cinnamon bun, coiled at the nape.

'I'm looking for something for my daughter for a trip,' Mom said.

The assistant's smile slipped. She pinned it back in

place on her face. I knew the look well. Salesgirls and me have a history. She looked at me now, wondering how to squeeze me into something that would fit my mother's sense of style.

'She looks like a very mature young lady,' she said.

And off we went, following her towards the back of the store. I was far too 'mature-looking' for Junior Miss. I wondered what 'she's a mature looking young lady' was in Spanish. My shame would translate.

Mom pushed another dress into the changing room. Some things never changed.

'How are you getting on? Don't force the zip. You need another size.'

Her voice peered through the curtain. It reminded me of the bus home from camp. For two minutes a year my mother looked hopeful. When the bus pulled in, I'd see her on tiptoe, watching me walk from the back seat. Moving from window to window to the front of the bus, my head and shoulders were all she could see. Anything was possible.

'Lovely to have you back!' she'd say, looking me up and down.

She'd pause, like she had to swallow the words her mouth wanted to say.

'Is that you? What happened to you? You look . . . '

We walked past parents using words we didn't use. Mothers hugged daughters, fathers hugged sons, amazed how little of their arms were needed to fit around.

Outside the changing room, my mother said, 'Twirl.'

I twirled. She stood back and frowned.

'Maybe something with a smock waist?' she said.

The salesgirl flitted away, dresses like failed parachutes in her arms.

If Mom could free me from camp, I could give her the sky on the plane. We switched seats so she could have the window. It was our first trip alone, other than weekends in Cape May – long days of Gramps on the boat, Gran trawling yard sales and Mom looking ashamed. Every night we met in the kitchen, Gran taking an interest in fishing in exchange for Gramps looking at the junk she'd bought, listening to the haggle of getting a dollar off, the drama of beating a neighbouring hand. I thought about their exchanges on the plane. Eating Mom's leftover chicken, I waited to hear 'Are you sure you aren't full?' It didn't come. If anything, she smiled a private smile, maybe the same way I sometimes could when she tilted the lilies in the vase. I took her giving me her cookie as a sign. I wanted to believe we could be friends.

The bus wound down the dizzying road to the hotel. Out of the window were pine trees I hadn't known Mexico had. I didn't know a lot. I could smell the pine, the orange of the Japanese man behind us, and the perfume of the woman in the seat in front, nursing a kid old enough to chew jerky. My mother had a million pictures of churches in her purse. She looked at them, determined not to look at the woman. Most of the passengers weren't American.

'San Cristóbal,' she'd said. Certain. 'Says here, it's popular with Europeans. I found out about something local we have to see. It's . . . ' She changed the subject to the hotel.

We got off the bus and took our passports to the desk to check in.

Mom held onto them with white fingers. 'Do we have to leave our passports?' she said. 'I have American Express.'

The clerk shook his sad head. We handed over our passports – two little faces in bad light.

'We can manage,' she said. 'Men can take things the wrong way,' she whispered, hauling our cases to our room.

The room was peach. Two beds, an iron table on the balcony and chairs with scrolled backs. My mother wiped the rail in the wardrobe before hanging our clothes. Then she laid stuff out on the bed to assemble a survival-kit tote: Spanish phrasebook, guidebook, traveller's cheques, handkerchiefs, toilet paper, toilet-seat covers, bottled water from home, pepper spray, Sweet'N Low.

'We have to smile, but not be too friendly,' she said, reading about women travelling alone.

I smiled, in a not-too-friendly way.

*

I kept a journal on vacation, though I was never the diary type. I hated the idea of my thoughts all in one place to be used as evidence against me sometime. Dad gave me a journal before we left. It had a bunch of blue and lilac stamps printed on the cover and a quote in typewriter print, *A traveller without observation is a bird without wings.* Dad had customised the pages inside. Under each day he wrote *Stuff I Liked, Stuff We Did, Stuff We Ate.* He gave it to me with a smirk, an acknowledgement passing from hand to hand.

Under *Stuff I Liked* I wrote: *The smell of cinnamon, mountain views, jack hares, markets, little tin things, red, bicycles, breakfast, the tile rose on the table, hot chocolate, raffia baskets, a whole family woven from corn on a craft stall, not knowing the language, being aware of my smile because it had to do all the work.*

Under *Stuff We Did* I wrote: *Walk, look, photograph old buildings, look in our phrasebook, sneeze, touch milagros, be afraid to haggle, smile, in a not-too-friendly way, say 'No thank you', say everything slower, tell taxi drivers we're on the way to meet Dad, walk away.*

Stuff We Ate had two columns, one for Mom, one for me.

Grapefruit	*Mexican Breakfast*
Coffee and cigarette	*Pozol*
Egg-white omelette	*Mole Chicken*
Orange Juice	*Pozol*
Grilled Fish	*Fish Tacos*

Banana & bran	*Burrito*
Coffee and cigarette	*Pozol*

Then, I got bored with Mom and just did my own. *Pozol* was like sippable chocolate popcorn. I had it at the hotel, in a café in the old square and from carts. On the street, my mother shaved off my milk moustache with her fingertip. I decided to add a new section to my book.

Stuff I Don't Like: My clothes laid out every morning like instructions of how to match Mom's purse. Hills. Cobblestones & Mom's heels. Mom's fork turning over every bite to spot food poisoning lurking beneath. The dummies in the Museum of Mayan Medicine – a midwife and a spread woman with no mouth. The long walk through unknown streets to get there, Mom's hand on the zipper of her purse, clutching her bottle of American water like Mace. (It reminded me of Eva and her Coke, a can in her hand all day. It stopped her fidgeting, she said. She missed it so bad at camp she poured water into an empty can, trying to trick herself.)

Most mornings, I took buses with my mother to small villages and lakes surrounding the town.

'Now this is what I had in mind,' Mom said.

People with backpacks shuffled off the bus like turtles with ill-fitting shells. Most wore slacks and took sloppy photos. They looked like they were saying, 'I was here,

next to this crumbling church. Ok, I looked sloppy – so what?' Outside the church in San Juan Chamula was a market crammed with pottery, woven blankets, paper Frida Kahlos and skeletons in red skirts. I touched strange *milagros*: tin fish and angels, the Virgin Mary, disembodied hearts, silver hands and feet that looked like they'd snap from the weight of a prayer. I wasn't sure what they meant, but I bought a stripy armadillo for Eva (a hard little shell). Mom beelined to a stall of hand-embroidered skirts, peasant blouses and lace shawls.

'Stand back,' she said.

I stood under the canopy. Two old women looked on, silently embroidering in wicker chairs behind the stall. My mother draped a shawl over my shoulders, and another on hers. Both were white lace, delicate feathers on our arms.

'Do you like it?' she said, combing fringes.

'I like this better,' I said.

I reached for a black one, embroidered with white flowers. She stroked the quality and picked up another covered in red roses, a garden on her back. She bought all four shawls, an embroidered and a lace one each. It was the first time she asked what I liked without saying I had no idea what suited me.

Back at the hotel, Mom wrote postcards to Dad and Ed. I started one for Eva at camp – I only needed two sentences, but none were right. What I wanted to send was a river of *pozol*, *tamales* like rafts. I wondered if Eva had managed to find a junior counsellor saving for college this year. There was always one, looking both ways, sliding down a zip in the boat shed, a duffle bag of Peanut Butter Cups, Butterfingers, Tootsie Rolls. Eva and I stared at plastic packets glistening like jewels in the half dark. The counsellor smiled the way shop assistants eyed our mothers in stores. 'This is a customer who knows what she wants. Take your time. Look. Anything else I can get you? No trouble at all.' Every night, Eva and I sat by the lake talking about our moms, eating chocolate with a mark-up to make them blush, laughing till we could burst a gut.

'You're peeling,' my mother said, rubbing lotion on my shoulders before bed. I thought about Eva peeling sunburn off my back at camp. She would hold up a mirror like a hairdresser showing a lady she was fit to go dancing. Carefully, I'd set about Eva's back, wishing we could just peel off a layer and reveal, underneath our old skin, the sort of daughters our moms could take on a trip.

It was Thursday when my Mom suggested we wear the white shawls. She got me up early, insisting I wear my best, and least comfortable, dress. I put it on. I still wanted to please her.

'Hannah, get a move on,' she said.

Her fingers twitched as if looking for lilies. She tucked my hair behind my ear. I didn't see what the big deal was. I'd had my fill of ruins, mountains and villages. Tomorrow we were spending the day in San Cristóbal doing last-minute shopping before our flight. Suddenly, my mother looked as eager as the morning of the sale at Bloomingdale's. This village wasn't in the guidebook, she said. No tour buses went from the square, all she had was a slip of paper with how to get there. Outside the old cinema, we rammed ourselves into a *colectivo* – a van full of backpackers and locals. The driver's music was deafening. The van jerked to a stop outside fields to let people on and off. We got off at a dirt track surrounded by corn.

'This way,' my mother said, looking at her map.

'Where we going?'

'You'll see,' she said.

I think she was smiling. Later, I wanted to remember if she was smiling so bad it hurt. I hoped we weren't visiting another old church: pretty as they were, they didn't mean more to me than an hour in the shade. Walking around them, my mother looked sort of bored, revived only when she saw tiles or woodwork that would look great at the summer house she was trying to persuade Dad to buy. I followed her uphill now, stopping to sip water and whine about the bugs picnicking on my arms.

'There's nothing here,' I said.

I looked around at cattle sheds, the odd house with a rickety tile roof.

'Here,' she said, 'I think.'

I panted behind her towards a white stone house. A skinny guy stood leaning against the wall, watching us approach. My mother took a handkerchief out of her purse and wiped the dust from our shoes. The man walked towards us, not smiling, just watching our clean shoes.

'Hello. Is this the right place? We're here to see, we heard . . . '

My mother fumbled in her purse, digging for her phrasebook, buried under breath mints and flyers.

The man nodded and held out his hand, palm to the sky.

'Yes, of course.'

She handed him pesos, I'm not sure how many, and we followed him into the house.

'Here? Thank you.'

My mother zipped her bag closed over her camera, like she did before we went into churches.

'What is this? Some cheese-making place or something?'

'Sshhh,' she said.

We stepped into a narrow hallway. My mother's hand rested on my back. Someone, an old woman, was coming out of the door at the end of the dim hall, rubbing her eyes. I squeezed in my stomach to let her pass. She stopped right in front of us and, cupping my cheek with the walnut of her hand, she cried, '*Señorita gorda encantadora. Señorita gorda encantadora.*' There were tears in her eyes. I stared at her lips, like a drawstring bag, tightened around contents I couldn't recognise.

'*Bendígale. Bendígale,*' she said.

She rushed past us to cry at the unsmiling man outside. My mother nudged me through the door at the end of the corridor and I lurched into the room. It was bare. A girl lay on an iron bed. In the corner was a woman on a chair. She stood, her hand gesturing us to the bed. She spoke in short bursts.

'Look,' she said, 'my daughter. She not eat since year of too much rain. Crops fail. Only small water touch her tongue for two years. Yet she alive. Is miracle. She a saint, everyone say.'

Her English was as bare as the room. She made a cross with her fingers over her shoulders and head. My mother followed, dabbing on a cross like perfume. I don't know why, but I did the same. I stared at the girl asleep in the bed, the light from the shutters making gold bars across her pale face. Her eyes were closed, her eyelids dark. I could hear her breathing, I thought. The white sheet, pulled up to the neck, barely moved.

The mother lifted the sheet for us to see stick legs, twig arms poking out of a white nightdress. Through it,

I could see ribs, frail as a house of matchsticks it looked like a sigh could blow down.

'We lost cattle. Corn. My daughter dream about angel. She know she did not have to eat,' the woman said.

My mother nodded as if she understood. Something about the woman looked proud. My cheeks burned hot and red. I stared at the girl, then the mothers. Why? I wanted to yell, Why are we here? What good does it do? How can this happen? Who let it? Who would it save? I looked up at the shutters and had the urge to throw them back, let sun flood the room, drown us all. I wanted to grab my mother's purse and drop mints in the girl's mouth one by one, feed her like a bird. I glared at my mother, opened my mouth and not a word came. I was close to the bed. I couldn't move. My hand touched the back of the hand of the girl, so cool it washed the heat from my own.

'Thank you,' my mother said. 'Bless you.'

The words were alien, spoken like a child repeating something it didn't know the meaning of, but wanted to know. The mother of the girl looked at me and patted my mother's hand. The door opened then, and the skinny man and a boy with crutches came into the room. My mother and I stepped into the slim hall, following the jangle of coins in the man's pocket outside.

Traipsing down the hill, my mother said we were lucky to see a miracle, a living miracle, in our lives. Even if it wasn't a miracle, they believed it, she babbled, they really believe.

'How many people can say that?' she said, opening her purse to take a picture of a farmer skinning a duck, that little extra bit of local colour rammed into her purse.

I didn't speak. I walked behind her, sun strapped to my back, our shadows swallowing each other if we got too close.

'We have to hurry,' she said, sipping water. She handed me the bottle. I shook my head, refusing the breath mints she offered. I just marched on, downhill towards the *colectivo*, the village, a little gift shop in town where we found a plastic money box of some saint with pink paint smeared on her lips and a slot in her crown.

'Your gran would love this!' Mom said. She combed tangled fringes on my shawl. 'Is there anything you want?'

I shook my head. No. There was not.

SHINE ON

The shop is all about rabbits, ladybirds and drifts of blankets so soft I want to bury myself in the folds. There's barely time to be here, I know. The visit's at four. I've cleaned, but nothing smells of lemons. I'm out of furniture polish and I haven't been able to shine for days. I'm aching to shine, even for a second, so I drag my friends to Babylove to concentrate. Blake's laughing. Shania sucks a frozen lolly like a Sex Ed teacher gone rogue. It's October, but that doesn't stop her. Once, I saw her buy ice cream in the snow like she was daring herself to feel all of the cold.

'No one taught us this at school,' Shania says, draining red colouring from the lolly. She grins, all stained mouth and white ice.

I say ssshhh, but not loud. It's a ssshhh for me only, like the hush I get inside whenever I come here. We blurt into the store and the door makes an alarmed drone. The woman arranging sippy cups looks like she'd prefer a proper silver bell. She says, 'Can I help you?' like she's breathed in a fly on her morning run. I say I'm just looking and browse like I'm loaded. Shania and Blake hit the breast pumps, howling. I pick up a blanket and can't see them. I'm all about soft fleece, the silk wings of a bumblebee embroidered above the hem. I close my eyes to shine in on Kensay, baby fingers flicker and fade. The shine is like a torch with duff batteries, I'm all off. The girls laugh me out of the zone. Blake's holding up a snowsuit. I picture Kensay in a chrome pram like a miniature Formula One driver and long to shine again. Blake asks if I'm alright, looking at me funny, like the time I told her about the shine, or tried to.

We were better friends between boyfriends. Me and Stan had split up, and Blake got dumped by the guy from the garage. In her bedroom, Blake dragged out her Love Book – folded card nicked from art, hole-punched spine. Each page listed the progress of love. *February – first time we kissed. March – first time you called me your girlfriend. April – first time we got jealous, first time we punched a wall. May – first time you proposed.*

'Are you ever with him when you're not there?' I asked.

'You mean like online?' said Blake, playing with her eyelashes like a butterfly had landed on her fingers. I could never stick them on straight.

'Close your eyes,' I said, 'and shine in on where he is now, what he's doing.'

Blake blinked, her eyes opened that fast. She didn't want to imagine anything, in case she imagined stuff no one needs to see. I tried to tell her to not imagine, just *see*. She replied, 'You're even crazier than me.' And I couldn't say anything about the shine, how even not seeing Stan, I saw him every day. Strangely, it was easier to shine for him then than now, like I just did what I had to. The social worker filled in forms. I stared at her defeated umbrella and was elsewhere. I didn't even have to close my eyes. I *saw* Stan peel rubber off his trainers in his room as if he was just lying around, missing me like a full-time job. Then, I shone in on Kensay, crying at a milk bottle because it wasn't me. It made me feel better somehow.

Blake waves a hand across my face, asking me something about snowsuits. I hold on to the bumblebee blanket.

'You can buy me it when I have the party,' I say. Shania yawns, she's heard all about the party. I want it to be like an American shower, a coo of girls handing me bibs and silk booties. They'll say Kensay is beautiful and looks nothing like me, and I'll call them all cows, but I'll laugh. I'll laugh all night long when I get the baby back.

The shop owner's pretending there's some sort of rabbit onesie display crisis behind us, so I place the blanket back, folding over a smear of lipstick on the fleece.

I didn't know I'd held it so close. It smelled of nothing but the plastic tag.

I'm thinking nothing but lemon furniture polish outside. The house doesn't have that lemony waft. I imagine the social worker, who's told me a dozen times to call her Anne, sniffing something missing, my utter lack of lemons, and mentioning adoption again. One of Shania's hands reaches into her bag and whips out a Peter Rabbit sippy cup. Blake emotes at plastic, 'Awwww.'

'Look, I got this for you,' Shania grins.

I give her the death stare that has no effect but to make Blake look sad.

'If you're going to do that stuff, don't drag me into it!' I say. 'What if I got caught? If I . . . '

Blake tugs her lip. Somewhere along the line of our friendship she's become the one who'd do the feeling bad for us all. Shania's all huffy. 'I didn't nick it!' she says. 'I bought you it last week!' Blake goes to link her arm in mine, like she wants to remind me of when we were younger and could argue and forgive each other every day. I grab the Peter Rabbit sippy cup and walk off, already planning an *I'm sorry, but* text. The *but* is the baby, and me being fifteen when I had her, and falling out with Mum and stuff. *But* is a lot of stuff, but it's not me now. I walk home past a woman with a buggy and wish I could shine in on wherever she's going, absorb her motherliness, but I can't shine on strangers. I've tried. I've sat in exams and closed my eyes, willing myself right there, seeing what the clever girls see. That paper, full of the right answers laid out before me.

It's supposed to be daytime, but the moon's out, chalking a faint idea of night onto the afternoon sky. I want to shine on Kensay, bad, but all I can see is a hundred things I must do like a sum that adds up to only one answer: fit. This afternoon, at 4pm, someone will say it about me, all mumsy cardigan and apple shampoo smell seeping out of me. The place will be immaculate. Stan and I will sit holding hands like a matching set of something: parents. I message him a reminder to come in a shirt, say I've got him a tie. Everything's going to be fit.

I'm marching back as fast as I can, but I can't step away from the look on Shania and Blake's faces. It's too soon to say I'm sorry. I shine in on her to see if she's ok.

Blake and Shania are in Girls' World considering hair extensions like Goldilocks'. There's a bad cover of a Bryan Adams song on. The security guard is cute, in a Bruce Willis way.

Shania's saying, 'I know she's our friend, but I don't know what to say to her any more, she's like a social worker. I'm sick of getting dragged to that snooty shop! I bet she won't even get Kensay back, not in that dump, with that flatmate . . . '

'You're probably right,' Blake's saying, 'but we can't tell her.
You know what she's like.'
She strokes a lock of red hair like a pony, loops it on the rail.

I won't listen. I'll get Kensay back, and have a shower,
rubber-duck napkins, cupcakes and balloons. The cows
better learn to coo. I text Stan a reminder to bring his job
applications as I unlock my door. My flatmate Lila's bedroom door is closed and her coat's not on the hook. The
hall smells like a mouldering meadow and the rabbit's out
in the lounge. I'm not sure who brought it. I came home
one afternoon and found Lila and some bloke watching it
hop about on the carpet. I scoop the rabbit into its cage
and sweep up droppings, small bags and bits of foil. I
close my eyes to see Kensay again – *her small hand grasps
a cloth rabbit toy* and I see no more. My shine's blocked
as the kitchen window, like something shattered and
someone came in with chipboard, sealed off the view. I
have too much to do.

'Can't make it, babe,' Stan messages. 'I forgot, I've
got this job interview.'

I pick up the phone and shine for him while it rings.
*He is lying on a couch, video game in his hand, ashtray on the
floor. His flatmate passes him a skinny cigarette. Stan hits mute
on his phone.*

'What did you say to her?' *the flatmate is saying.*

'Interview,' Stan inhales the word. Smoke and resignation curl in the air. 'What's the point going? Just for someone to say she won't get the baby back?'

I call it my shine because I don't have another name for it. The closest I've seen is that movie kid in an icy hotel. He shines and the caretaker comes. I shine, and it's not like that at all. I can't communicate a thing, I just see what someone else sees, listen, inhale someone else's life for a minute. It's not that useful; it wasn't to my mum. She knew where I'd been, why I was late, shining on me every night like a spy. I won't phone.

Mum is pulling a T-shirt down over her muffin-top and re-arranging the furniture, the same as last time I looked in. The living room is orange. It was purple last year. She's dissatisfied with the placement of a chair. I see cotton flowers rolled into a corner, rolled out. There's a stain from my grilled Mars bar on toast phase on the arm.

I shine off. Let her do the shining. Let her call. Or not. We've witnessed each other in so many private moments neither of us knows what to say.

Ssshhh. The polish can puffs air at dust on the coffee table. I forgot to buy more. There isn't time now: the visit is in less than an hour and everything should smell of lemons, lemons could clinch it. It's quiet, but for a hum in the kitchen. I open the fridge. There's a bottle of cloudy lemonade in the door. The lid gasps. I pour lemonade onto a cloth and wipe the worktop, the sink, the TV, in the lounge. I can just about smell something like lemons, but not enough. I drench the cloth more, polish the coffee table and finally, breathing lemon, I feel I can shine. I see Kensay. Everything is so clear.

The baby is fussing in a white crib, biting her hand. Looking up, she sees penguins waddling around a mobile. The light is pale blue, arctic lit by a nightlight plugged in at the wall. The room is wide, fluffy carpeted, warm. On the shelves, on the walls, is what seems to be the whole contents of the swanky Babylove store: ladybird softies, a rabbit onesie, blankies. Kensay fusses some more. Ssshhh a woman is saying. Long fingers arrange blankets in the crib, silky bumblebees are embroidered above the hem, fleece soft as snow.

Sssshhh. The woman is picking Kensay up. Back and forth she walks, a ring on her finger like an iceberg.

'She just wanted a cuddle,' a man is saying. There's a smile to it, though I can't see it. Kensay is closing her sleepy eyes. Together, the man and woman back and forth and ssshhh.

And I can't be there any more. I lie back on the couch, knackered, and pour lemonade into the Peter Rabbit sippy cup. I sip and sip, sliding my feet onto the sticky coffee table that smells of lemonade.

WHEN WE WERE WITCHES

Mother craned from her chair. Two crows scraped their beaks on the stone ledge outside. She ran to the window, knocking over the vase on the sill. Off they flew, leaving scratchy bird feet in the snow.

'One for sorrow, two for joy,' she said.

She sat, then got up, listening to the morning. Knock kno– . . . She flung the door open, a leathery fist hovered midair.

'Come in.'

The witch came in without wiping her feet. I sat on the mat, inching behind the chair. The woman's skin was dried meat, withered. The top of her spine was a question mark.

'Is this the child?' She squinted at me the way women at the market squeeze peaches, getting a feel for a bad patch under the skin. I looked at the rug. I don't remember every rag in it. If I'd known, I'd have torn the colour of waistcoats and bodices from the mat, I'd have studied my mother, folded up the look on her face and put it in my pocket to read when I might understand it.

'Stand up,' the old woman said.

'Go on,' Mother said, 'it's best.'

I stood straight as a sunflower saluting the light. And, like a sunflower, I drooped, the curve of my spine refusing to let me stand as straight as I'd like. I crossed my legs, one foot in front of the other. The bad foot ballooned, still bigger than the other, whether I looked like a girl about to curtsy or not. The woman grabbed my hands, wiggled my fingers and turned my palms upside down.

'Nowt wrong there anyway,' she said.

'Can you take her?' Mother asked.

The woman nodded slowly, a burden weighting her pointy chin.

Mother grabbed the bundle of my clothes from under the chair. The witch took them, knotting her other hand around mine. I pulled away.

'Ssshhh. Don't fuss,' Mother whispered. 'Go, it's for your own good.'

Outside, snow landed on my hair like salt rubbed into meat for the pot. Clamped to the woman's hand, I walked down the path and looked back at the gate. *Don't make me go.* Mother had already closed the door.

We hobbled over cobbles, past houses with half-drawn curtains, out past the big house and into the woods. Our feet bit into snow, our breath was rags in the cold.

'Where we going?' I said. 'I want to go home.'

'We don't always get what we want,' the witch said, fingers twined.

I knew she was a witch. What else could she be? She was ancient and ugly and there was a devil's mark on her neck, a raisin of flesh. I'd heard what Mother's visitors said. Bundled into the box bed when anyone came, I pressed my ear to the door.

'Too much sickness,' a man said. 'Crops failing. Some reckon there's a witch in the woods cursing us all. They say she can turn people to stone.'

The woods thickened. The sun lowered, spinning our shadows spindly on the ground. Somewhere, I could hear water. The trees we passed now were scarred. Hanged men dangled, scratched onto the bark. I looked back, but I didn't run. It was some sort of spell, I was sure. I couldn't let go of the witch's hand. I remembered Mother closing the door: *Go*.

The house hunched in a clearing littered with stones. Looking close, I saw they weren't just stones. Each one *was* something, a sleeping cat dusted in white powder, a bird that looked as if it had been flying over the house and fell out of the sky. On the rickety porch was a row of children's clothes and small toys – all stone.

'Wipe your feet, girl,' she said.

I stamped into the house. Once a witch sets her eye on you there's nowhere to run – a girl's sugar and spice catches up with her in the end. The kitchen flickered with firelight. The smell of ginger cake drifted up my nose. And my stomach rumbled, obeyed. If the witch wanted to fatten me up, I was too hungry to resist. She took a knife and hacked a wedge of cake out of the tin on the range. I nibbled and sniffed, nibbled and sniffed. She handed me a cloth for my face. I was crying without making a sound, I knew no other way. *Ssshhh,* Mother always said, *don't fuss.*

What have you heard about a witch's house? Some of it's true. It was higgledy-piggledy with bottles and jars, and bunches of herbs dangled from the shelves. Everything looked put out to dry, a string of wizened toads stretched like bunting over the fire. I stared at an iron pot, big enough to make children's bone soup. The witch patted a fat chair. I sat, one eye on a cage by the door. It looked too small to fit in.

'Feet!' she said. She bent with a crack, mopping up clods of snow melting into water on the floor. I swallowed my last bite of cake and she began to unwind the leather wrapped around my feet. This was it. If she ate me, she was going to start at the toes.

'You never had proper shoes?' she asked, tossing wet leather at the fire. It sputtered and spat.

'Mother said it's best I don't go outside.'

She squeezed my bad foot. It was purple, bound tight to make it look smaller than it was.

'Does it hurt?' she asked.

'I don't know.'

I couldn't feel anything: my foot, my fear, Mother closing the door. The witch slopped water into a bowl and said, 'Plonk your feet in.' It was warm, steam sighed from my toes. When they were good and wrinkly she patted them dry and rubbed in something waxy-cold from a jar. I yawned, my eyes closing, refusing to keep an eye on her. She turned down the blankets of a small bed in the other room and tucked me in tight as a sausage in pastry. I slept well. All night I dreamed I was eating her house.

Porridge breathed on the wooden table. A jug of rosehip syrup sat next to it. I grabbed a spoon, poured and ate. Snap. Snap. Snap. A crunching outside like something wicked breaking bony necks. She came in, carrying sticks for the fire.

'Did you sleep well?' she asked.

I smacked sticky lips painted shiny by syrup. 'Yes.'

She nodded and laid a sheet of paper on the floor.

'Stand there,' she said.

She bent down and drew around my feet. The pencil tickled, but I didn't laugh. When she was done drawing, she cut out my paper footprints, laid one on a rabbit skin and started to stitch, pins in her lips.

'Try it,' she said, handing me the rabbit-skin boot.

I walked unevenly. One foot bare.

'How does it feel?'

'Soft. Warm.'

'Not too tight? I need more skin for the other foot,' she said, picking up the cage by the door.

The snow landed white, speckling her dark shawl as she set the trap. I stood in the doorway looking at the stones on the porch. One was shaped like a doll. One looked like a girl's bonnet, another was a small stone boot. I looked down at my bare foot beside the one covered in fur. I could try to run, run back to Mother, but not today. I'd wait until I had another rabbit foot, then I'd hop away.

Each morning we collected wood, set traps and hacked vegetables out of the frozen soil behind the house. I walked past the stone shoes and bonnet and shivered. The wind swept snow over the footprints of birds on the ground. Looking out at the woods, I was no longer sure which direction was home.

'You can eat,' she said, watching me lick a bowl clean. 'Well, the more you help out, the more food there is.'

And I did help. She chopped wood, I bundled sticks.

She kneaded bread, I greased the tin. She rolled pastry for me to squish frills around raven pies and apple tarts. The small house was jammed with mouth-watering smells. Sometimes I thought about my mother, then the witch laid out a tray of parkin. The sugary crust glistened, coating my fingertips in sticky gold. I ate until only my stomach ached.

Winter crumpled to spring, spring opened into summer. It was hot, the shhh splash of water washed my ears. I followed the witch with her pail. She held up one hand and took a knife from her boot.

'You can't go any further,' she said, carving a star onto an oak tree.

'Why not?'

'Too dangerous. There's a cliff where the water falls into a pond. Children who stray there are never seen again.'

'What happens to them?'

'No one's survived to tell. Some say they fall. They say the pond is the devil's mouth – chews you up.'

She chomped, showing several teeth.

The star carved into the oak wept sap. I waited for her to weave back through the trees, bent over the bucket, water sloshing on the grass.

'Don't just stand there, lass, give me a hand.'

*

The snap of a stick, the rusty gate. Who's that? Sometimes someone came to the house. Occasionally, they made it to the door, braving it past the stone cat and bird sleeping on the path. The witch got out the eggs and a jar full of crow feathers. She cracked shells to tell people their future, set fire to a feather and said, 'Your husband will not fly far from home.' Mostly, people came to cure a cough, make someone love them, or help them get to sleep. She crushed herbs into honey in a jar and accepted bags of flour and balls of twine from women with their worries packed into the bags under their eyes.

'Was that a spell?' I asked when they left.

'If a spell is making someone sleep easier and I get what I need for doing it . . . ' the witch said, whisking the fortune-telling eggs into omelette. 'Now, pass me the pepper.'

She smiled, putting her cackle back on the shelf with the feather jar. It didn't always stay there long. When a visitor told us about raised taxes, illness or failed crops in the village she got ready for business.

'Looks like we'll be run off our feet, lass,' she said, stitching chicken legs to a wild boar and letting it spit over the fire. She boiled sugar with blackberries, dipped in sweetbreads and left them to dry. I stuck little stalks into the tops. When the sugary purple coating was dry, I rubbed in the flour. I'd offer the purple fruit to our guests and watch their eyes grow, wide with amazement at the 'plum' that tasted of meat.

'"That witch has a tree that grows meat," they'll say. "She curses chickens into hideous beasts!"' she laughed. 'They'll be piddling themselves all the way home!'

'Why's that a good thing?' I asked.

'You're too young to know.'

With each year that passed, I learned a little more. She told me the benefits of each herb, and how to cure a rabbit skin, but nothing about herself.

'Were you always a witch?' I asked. 'When you were little, did you roll down hills and get grass in your hair? Were you like me?'

'I was never little,' she said, laying a cold hand on my fever. She folded a wet cloth onto my head, smoothing away sticky strands of hair. I shivered under a deerskin, soup-filled and sick. I patted her hand. She pulled away like it stung.

'Sooner you're better, sooner you start pulling your weight around here,' she said.

Her scowl was too late. I'd already seen something that on a pretty lady would have looked like kindness. Over the years, I saw it sometimes, a glimpse of worry, amusement or pride at something I did. There, on her face, then snatched away.

The year I turned fourteen, I was sure I'd imagined it. The woman wasn't kind. One day at a time, she was turning me from a girl into a witch. And I hated it. Everyone knew what happened to witches. Warts and moles sometimes came to the house attached to women afraid of someone getting the wrong idea. The witch poked warts with a flame, and they let her, less scared of the pain than what could happen otherwise. Yet still she talked about me the way she did.

'Don't look directly at the lass, she might give you the evil eye. When she was a baby she flew out of her crib. The devil's playmate, born on a full moon.'

I looked down, cheeks burning. No one would look me in the eye.

'Careful. If she doesn't like the look of you, she'll turn you stone,' the witch said.

The stammering boy who came for a love spell dropped his smile and raced down the path past the stone birds, cats and clothes.

'Why did you say that?' I asked.

'He'll be running home telling stories,' she grinned. '"Sin ugly," he'll say. "If you touch that lass, she'll petrify your hand."'

I gave her the sort of look people supposed would turn them to stone. As soon as spring came I'd run away.

*

Orange leaves were frosted to the grass. A slight woman crunched to the door in a rustling skirt. I looked out. Mother! Mother was coming to take me home, after all these years, just when I most wanted to go. The woman knocked, I ran, a half-limp, half-run. She was young, ash-blond wisps of hair frayed out of her bonnet like smoke. I could hardly recall my mother, but this wasn't her. This woman was barely more than a girl. She held an infant in her arms.

'Will you help me?' she said. 'Look.' She unwrapped the infant's sheet and held up his arm. Six fingers curled on one hand.

'Can you do something?' she said.

Even for a visitor, the old woman didn't get out her cackle and hiss. Extending a finger, she stroked a small bump of bone on the baby's forehead and sighed. She looked more woman than witch.

'It's a third eye! Fix him,' the young woman said, 'please.'

'There's nothing I can do.'

'You take him, then. I can't keep him like this. People will . . . '

She pushed the baby towards the witch. The witch folded her arms, not taking a thing.

'You're his mother,' she said. 'You need to do right by him.'

The woman cried then nodded. Holding the infant,

she left with a whisper. 'It'll be alright, I know I can make everything be alright somehow.'

We found the bundle out in the woods. The white sheet stuck hard to the frost, the witch peeled it off the ground with a crack.

'Not a pick on him,' she said, holding the infant in her wrinkled hands.

'Shall we bury him?' I asked.

She shook her head, the way she did when we found the dead feral cat. And like the cat, she walked away now, towards the sound of the water, cradling the cold baby in her arms.

'Get on with the kindling, lass,' she said.

She weaved past the tree I was forbidden from straying beyond. I stroked the moss on the star carved into the bark and followed as quietly as I could.

The water hissed, throwing itself over the precipice, hammering the rocks in the pool. The witch placed the infant in the pool. I moved closer, my rabbit-skin feet crushing frosty leaves. She turned sharply, listening, always listening for footsteps. She saw me approach and didn't say a word.

I stood beside her, looking up at the waterfall. The ivy on the rocks was green where no water touched it. Further down, splashed by falling water, it was white.

Dandelions clung to holes in the cliff face, their flowers pale as bones.

'It's the water; something in the ground makes everything it touches turn to stone,' she said, dipping a hand in the water and looking at her wet palm. No different to any other woman's hand, just older. 'It takes time, drop upon drop, year after year.'

'Did anyone ever fall into the water and disappear?' I asked.

'No.'

I looked down at pale shapes in the water. The feral cat freckled in lime. The cloth doll I once cuddled, its button eyes now stone.

'Everything was here? The bird, the shoes near the house . . . '

'You know any other way to make people think you can turn them to stone?' she said.

I didn't. For years I'd looked away whenever I passed the small stone clothes and toys outside the house, afraid to ask where they came from. I didn't want to know.

'Come,' she said. She walked around the cliff face to a crack in the rock. It was dim, water seeped and dripped into the cave onto several large rocks, all chalk white. The witch walked among them, stroking each. One was a girl asleep. One hand bigger than the other, her palms were together, pressing a prayer to her cheek. Beside her, a younger girl sat hugging her knees, one hand with six fingers clutching creases in her skirt ironed into place by lime. Everywhere, there were imperfect children – all stone.

'You're not the first girl I took in,' the witch said. 'Their mothers were fallen, simple, superstitious. They asked me to cure their cursed children. And when I couldn't . . . '

'You took them in to make them witches?' I said.

She rubbed her head like it ached.

'There's two ways to be a witch, lass. You can not know it until they come with torches, or you can be ready. If folk fear you enough, they won't touch you. Come plague or taxes, when people look for someone to blame, you'll be safe.'

She ran a hand over stone tangles on the sleeping girl's head. 'It's not much of a life, being a witch, but it's a life,' she said. 'I did all I could.'

'What happened to them?'

'I didn't do enough. Some died in the woods trying to escape, others got older and lonely for love. They wasted away. They were witches who just wanted to be girls.'

I thought of how she never held me as a child, all the times she snatched her hand away. I was like that feral cat she left food out for but never spoke a good word about. She knew he could go at any time.

'Why didn't you ever tell me?' I said, looking around at the stone girls: so many clubbed feet, crooked spines and small hands like mine.

'How could I?' she said. 'How?'

EVERYWHERE YOU DON'T WANT TO BE

I saw the other me on a rainy morning – at least, I did the first time. The city dripped and surged. Everything smelt of wet dog. She was huddled in the doorway of a pawnbroker's with a bin bag and a blanket. Her voice creaked when anyone passed by.

'Spare change?' she asked a guy in a suit. 'Spare change?' she asked the jogger with the bouncy ponytail.

I was walking to work balancing coffee. I averted my eyes from her, loath to see.

'Nice shoes,' she said.

I looked down at my shoes, and glanced across. She was familiar, sort of. I supposed I'd passed her before. She wore a baseball cap and a coat like a half-inflated life raft. She was filthy and had a scar on her cheek; there was nothing remarkable about her. Some people all sort of look alike. In the morning I saw her again. *Spare change. Spare change. Spare . . .* People rushed. Men with newspapers tossed coins.

'Nice bag . . . real nice,' she said to me.

Something in her voice bugged me. Mocking, judge-mental even. My fingers rubbed the phone in my pocket. Silent. Still. I stormed on, then doubled back.

'Why don't you ever ask *me* for change?' I demanded.

I glared into blue eyes, sort of like my mother's, but hard as frozen water.

'You? You never gave me shit.'

She laughed, then coughed. Laugh, cough, laugh, cough. Who was she to judge? It was one of those moments when everything that's wrong in the world took the form of one person, one old woman in a doorway with the wrong tone.

'You don't know I wouldn't give you money,' I said.

'Of course I know. You only give to guys with dogs. Sometimes buskers, if they're cute.'

She was right. I rifled for change, finding only cash cards and gum. I tossed the gum at her like some sort of horrible-woman repellent and ran.

'See you soon, Zoe,' she called after me.

Not if I saw her first.

It hadn't been long since my birthday, not that it matters. It was all good, as they say. Christian sent yellow roses. It was a sign. I'd been seeing him for months, off and on, but the flowers had to mean something, if nothing more than 'I'm sending you flowers'. It's a start.

'Happy birthday,' he said.

'Thanks for the roses.'

'Now, if you want your *real* present . . . ' He took my hand and tilted his head towards the restaurant door. I knew what he meant.

The rain mizzled out. Drops clung to ledges of buildings. Wobbled. Dropped. I stepped out for lunch. How did that old woman know my name? I was sure I'd misheard. I'd decided to switch my panini supplier from the café with the steel tables outside to the sandwich shop with the hippo on the sign, just in case. I turned right instead of left. I was waiting to hear from Christian (*Status: In a relationship*, without a name.) Instead, I got a message from Louise.

Once, Louise and I had shared a flat at the bottom of a hill. Nappies flowed down the drains from the big houses. Ours were blocked. We peered into the manhole outside like sisters at a rock pool, narrowed voices tunnelling underground, swimming away from us like silvery fish. I held a net on a stick of bamboo. Louise looked down beside me.

'What do you think's down there?' she asked.

'Could be anything: alligators, drugs, CHUDs,' I said.

'Wouldn't it be cool if we fished out a tiny mermaid?'

'Like a goldfish? Yeah, I bet people flush mermaids all the time.'

The net scooped up wet wipes, but for a moment we were catchers of mermaids, the only two people in the world fishing a drain who wouldn't have been too surprised to find a shitty little mermaid on our hands.

I stared at the text from Louise. I only heard from her now when she wanted something. She was moving house and wanted someone to carry her shit. The phone felt heavy in my pocket. So many people carried around all day. Where was Christian? I hadn't heard from him since . . . I stepped under the scaffolding in front of the pizza shop. And there she was again, the homeless woman, everywhere you don't want to be, and on me in a heartbeat.

'He's not going to call,' she said. 'Tosser.'

She sat with her back to the cushion of a bin bag, an empty burger carton on the floor freckled with copper and silver at her feet. I glanced at my phone, just Josh dressed like Thor. *Gotta love a guy with a hammer?* (*Status: Nice guy, train wreck of a wardrobe, unfortunate goatee, good in bed.*) Pending reply: smiley face – the *yeah, whatever* of our age. Josh wasn't who I was waiting for. I put the phone away, staring at the woman, eyes the colour of mine, that nose. I recognised it, I recognised her. The bag lady. It was horrible. She looked just like me. She *was* me, in how many years' time? I gripped my phone, waiting for a ring to wave in her face. Not a peep.

'All the leaves are brown, and the sky is grey . . . ' she started to sing as I walked away. 'I went for a waaa . . . '

Cough. Sing. Cough. She was singing my ringtone, a throat full of rusty autumn leaves.

So, this is what thirty-three feels like. Birthday cards jostled over the fireplace. Seven. If I was a maths person I'd work it out. One card = one friend retained per X amount of years of my life, but I'm not a numbers person really. My wall online was full of greetings from strangers. Roses were starting to unclench in the vase. I took off the same shirt I had worn at thirty-two, got in the bath and placed the phone on the wire rack near the shampoo. Christian was away at a wedding. The invite included a plus one.

'We never said this was serious,' he said. 'Not going to a wedding serious anyhow.'

How serious did we have be to watch other people cut cake? Seriou*ser*, apparently.

'No biggie. Weddings are boring anyway,' I said.

I recalled my mother's weddings: his side, her side, nervous smiles, glances across the divide. I didn't want to go to a wedding – I just didn't want to be someone he didn't want to take to one. Washing my hair, I pictured the beggar woman's cap. Is this the sort of shit she thought? Did this shit make her wind up where she was? God, I was nothing like her. I wasn't. The bath fizzed with raspberry bath-bombs. I had decent shampoo. Drying my hands, I picked up the phone and hit *Christian. Thinking of you*. God no. Backspace. Delete. The beggar woman's laugh rattled in my soapy ears. I started typing again. *How are you?* Delete. Boring. *I miss you*. Delete. *In the bath, thinking of you*. That'd do it, dilute the sentiment with nakedness. Send. Count to sixty. One elephant. Two elephant. Christian replied when I got to fifty-one elephants.

Yeah? What you thinking? What you doing?

Pumicing my feet. I put down the stone and typed what he'd like to hear. Somewhere he was reading it. For minutes, the other numbers on his phone didn't exist.

I didn't have to go there, but I did. I took clothes off the radiator and pictured the other me outside. Freezing. If I left her out in the cold, I could be killing myself. I buttoned my coat and stepped outside. The road sparkled with frost. Everything looked sharp, metallic. I got in the car and drove.

I found myself outside the pawnbroker's in town. She was curled under a purple blanket in the doorway. I cranked the car window down.

'Get in,' I yelled.

She didn't move.

'Get in.'

The blanket twitched. She turned around.

'What?'

She sounded like I'd caught her in the middle of something, like she had a hundred and one things to dream.

'What do *you* want?'

'I don't know,' I said.

She knotted her bag and rustled to the car. The seatbelt stretched over woman and bag. I drove, sniffing fries on her hair, vinegary fingers and the warm stale smell of beer fermenting under her skin.

I opened my door and she marched straight to the kitchen, opened the cupboard and took out the cereal. She ate from the box, shovelling Rice Krispies in her mouth.

'Milk?' I asked.

She shrugged the way I did when I was thirteen, so articulately, a *whatever* tilt of her head. I sat the milk down. She poured and lowered her ear, listening to the snap, crackle and pop.

'Would you like something hot?' I said. 'I could make soup.'

I opened a can of tomato and slugged it in a pan. 'Take off your coat.'

I wouldn't ask her to make herself at home. No. Don't. She cuddled into her coat like I was planning to steal it. I wondered how many layers she had, if she was fat or just dressed all-terrain.

'Cut the crap,' she said.

I expected the other me to be grateful I'd let her in, but my only thanks was a belch that billowed from her milk-covered mouth.

'How many shite cans of soup you gonna try to feed me till you ask what you want? Soup? That's why you brought me here? Who you fucking kidding?'

She took a hanky from her pocket and made a raking sound in her throat. There was so much I had to ask her. Where did I go wrong? Why am I you? But I was damned if I'd ask now and prove she knew what I was thinking. I poured the soup, glancing sideways. She had that small mole on her chin and, looking close, that tiny hole from an old piercing under her lip.

'When did you start swearing all the time?' I asked.

She spoke nothing like me, I was sure of that at least. I'd turned down the music on the party in my mouth for my first job. I couldn't imagine why I'd let it blare up again, all those conversational shits and fucks.

'That's for me to know,' she said. 'No bread? Typical. Why do you have a shiny toaster when you never have bread?'

She sprinkled Rice Krispies onto her soup. Slurped. I could see this wasn't going to be easy. Now the other me was here I didn't know how to talk to her.

'How did this happen? You know, you ending up . . . '

'A manky old ragbag?' she said.

'I wasn't going to say that.'

'Course not, you'd have pussyfooted around, full of shit.'

She laughed again, the ghost of the laugh I had stealing my stepsister's doll when I was eight and throwing it onto the shed roof.

'Well? How did you get like this?'

'I'm tired,' she said, licking drips off the bowl, red soupy trails.

'Of course. I'll get some blankets and make up the couch.'

'You have a spare room.'

'Well, yeah, but it's a mess, it would take me too long to sort it.'

'Bollocks,' she said. 'You just don't want me stinking up your snazzy new sheets.'

She knew me way too fucking well.

I lay in bed, rubbing in moisturiser. 'Vanishing cream', my mother used to call it. I wondered if she had met herself too, if she'd had a crazy old woman of her own to make disappear. I listened to downstairs, I could hear snoring. The other me didn't seem to need the TV on to get to sleep. Did I snore? I sounded like a motorbike revving up to drive through the house, knock down the paper-thin walls.

The blankets were gone from the couch in the morning. The bitch robbed me, I bet. I pictured her filling her sack, stealing all my stuff, like some sort of anti-Santa. I didn't know her well. Who knows what they're capable of? I rushed to my bag – cash cards intact, nothing missing that I could see. I opened the front door. She was stood on my path, the white wool throw off the couch poking out of her bag.

'Spare change?' she said, hand out to the neighbours.

The couple next door looked away, turning back to give me a look. Bastards. You can't tell who's a good person by whether or not they recycle. How you do tell? I still didn't know – the other me wouldn't say.

I tugged her begging arm. 'You can't do that.'

'Why not?'

'They're my neighbours. I see them everyday. It looks bad.'

'Ah, yeah, I forgot. It's *so* important how everything looks.'

Inside, I made porridge. The woman clawed through the cupboard, tossing glazed cherries into her bowl like bombs.

'How can you do it?' I asked.

'Do what?'

'Beg. I'd *never* do that.'

'You sure?'

She grinned missing teeth. Beep. Christian. *Can't make tonight. No biggie. Catch you next week?* The woman sniffed.

'Do you remember Christian?' I said. 'Did you love him?'

She folded her arms, saying nothing. I wondered how to make her to leave.

'You can have a bath before you go if you like,' I said. 'I'll get you some clean clothes.'

I wasn't sure I had anything that might fit. Maybe sweatpants, or the cardigan I'd bought for my mother that last Christmas. I went upstairs, brushed my teeth again and brought it down.

'Try it on.'

'Thought you didn't want to end up anything like your mother?' she grinned.

That gap in her teeth again. Try that new toothpaste, I reminded myself.

I wondered what the other me was doing all day in my house while I was working. I didn't want to leave her, but she didn't seem to be going anywhere fast. 'Don't you trust yourself?' she laughed. I considered how to make her disappear. I texted almost everyone I knew just to ask how they were, like buying an insurance policy. I couldn't be that woman if I had someone. Could I? I swirled my keys walking to my front door. I was sure I'd find myself knitting with an old lady smile. Maybe she'd be doing Pilates, or off somewhere on a Caribbean cruise, just wouldn't be here at all.

She was crossed-legged on the floor holding the phone.

'Get a proper job, you gobshite.'

Slam.

'Who was that?'

'Telemarketers,' she said.

'I got bread.' I held up the bag.

'That's not bread, it's shite,' she said, squeezing the diet loaf out of my hands. 'You never call things what they are.'

The phone trilled in the hall. Josh wanted me for the pub quiz. Why not? I wandered back into the lounge.

'Do you want a baked potato?' I asked.

I looked around the room. No sign of me, but a squished bit in the loaf, slowly expanding back into shape.

There was a cool moon outside. Crisp, not a cloud. There were shopping lists on the backs of my birthday cards; all that was left of the roses was a ribbon on a stick. Christian had told me he wanted to keep things casual. And I was sleeping with Josh again to kill time. I sprayed on perfume to meet him at the pub quiz. Then it came. *Bored. Wanna come round?* Christian. I read the message, unsure whether to cancel my plans. It could mean something, it could change everything. Out of the window, I caught a glimpse of the old woman wandering down the street. I raced out with the phone in my hand.

'Tell me something, please,' I said, waving the phone.

She glanced at me, walking on.

'Tell me what to do, please.'

She stopped and leaned in as if she might kiss me. I waited, inhaling beer and something surprising, like soap.

'Do you want to know something? I'll tell you . . . '

Her voice was husky, a whisper. I leaned so close our noses touched like Eskimos.

'Fuck off,' she yelled, her breath punching me in the face.

Already, she was walking away, moving faster than it looked like she could, cuddling her sack.

'I'll go to the cash machine, I'll give you whatever you like, just fucking tell me something.'

I was chasing her now in my stupid blue heels. I slipped on the path one step behind her and got up picking something out of my face, a bit of smashed glass from the street. I stared at my wet fingers, dark, blood like ink under the moon. The old woman rustled back, pulling something woolly from her sack. She knelt and held a sock to my face.

'It's not so bad,' she said. 'See? It could be worse.'

She pointed to a silvery scar on her cheek, a whisker of white under the streetlight. We sat on the kerb side by side, waiting for the bleeding to stop, just looking up at the sky. She stroked next door's cat and got up.

'See ya,' she said.

I watched her get smaller walking down the street towards . . . who knew what? The phone trembled in my palm. *Got plans*, I typed. I still don't know if it was the right reply or not, what those two small words could mean, the brush stroke they made, or didn't, in the bigger picture of my life. I'd like to say the other me disappeared for ever as soon as I did it, but that's a crock. Let's just say I didn't see her for a while, and when I did we just sat, silentish. Still.

DOG YEARS

Life as a Dog-Faced Girl

It's not so bad being a dog-faced girl, even a stray. Scared I'd bite the superstitious hand of the village, my mother left me to the nuns. My birth certificate is a sideshow flyer. It says Momma saw a man eaten by a wolf when her belly was a full moon. Then I was born, hairy. I imagine she's howling somewhere.

~

In the orphanage Sister Bernadette tells me stories about Saint Wilgefortis, who grew a beard to avoid marrying an unbeliever. Fur has its uses, though she dies at the end.

I squeeze the doll she made me – a little stuffed dog wearing a peach dress. It's like me, has a smile stitched to its fur.

~

Someone travels to meet me. I'm talented, he says, my talent's just being myself. And that's rare. The nuns kiss me goodbye, lips light as moths' wings. Mr Barthley clips a lock of fur off my cheek for Sister Bernadette to remember me by. For anyone else, he says, he'd charge a buck.

~

On stage, I wear lace. A spotlight shines through it to poke at the fur. I sing love songs. Everyone laughs, except one man.

'Scam. She's not real! She's wearing a mask.'

Mr Barthley shouts back, 'Defamation of character! I'll sue.'

He pays the man later for getting us in the newspaper again.

I touch my cheek, trying to find the edges of my mask, peel the look off my face.

~

I share a trailer with a tattooed lady with an inkless face. She wears long sleeves to town, brings back perfume samples and cake. I don't go myself. Once, at night, I went to the beach and made a mermaid of sand. If I sunbathe the circus will fold. I'm sacred as a cow. No one need buy my milk if I leak it for free.

There's always circus boys.

~

Every day I don't see the lobster boy is seven years. Archie has beautifully smooth arms. He does everything with stumps so gracefully; my hands are paws. I sniff around his trailer. Outside Archie rolls a cigarette, flips it to his lips.

'Hi.'

I whimper. These days I feel more dog than girl. Even my imagination is loyal; I can't imagine anyone else loving me.

~

I ask the mirror if I'm pretty. My fur is impressive, people say. I'm not sure it's the same. The razor winks at the sun. I shave, dab my face and tie ribbons in my hair. Furless, I'm silver, a ghost. I don't look like me. I walk to Archie's with candy, ready for him to drop his tobacco, beg a kiss.

'Dog girl?' he says. Then he yells, 'Check this out! She won't be able to work for a month! Roll up, roll up. See the world's dumbest girl!'

Lobster laughter scuttles back to my mirror behind me. It's not so bad being a dog girl – it'll be harder to be a dog-faced woman, I feel.

THE KEEPER OF THE JACKALOPES

The best bit is the bit that used to scare her. Once the skin has been removed, the rabbit lies on the table without its bunny suit on. It can be anything it wants. Clary strokes the cool fur. The bench is covered in wire and wood wool. The pieces are all laid out. Her father stares at the clay skull with a finger on his chin, ready to put the rabbit back together again. Clary watches him, recalling when there weren't any rabbits, only jackalopes popping up like magic. He'd cover each with a box until it was perfect. Then she'd lift the cardboard. There it was. The jackalope. Antlers, ears, rabbity whiskers almost twitching on her fingers. It looked like it was about to hop off, and got frozen with the horizon in its eyes.

The window lets in a strip of air thin as memory. Clary pours coffee. One for him. One for her: half milk, half coffee, one sugar per foot she has grown in the last few years. The footsteps on the walkway are curt. Each rap on the door is perfectly spaced, like someone learned at college how to knock right, what every knock means. Clary answers the door, nudging the dent on the frame with her hip. The man's shirt is cornflower. He rolls up his sleeves without looking, just rolling, rolling his way through the day. He looks at Clary, adjusts his silky tie and fails to adjust what to say. Whether the girl is tall, wearing tight yellow shorts and has a fake tattoo of a chipmunk on her wrist, or not, he asks, 'Is your mommy or daddy home?' He frowns at the magic marker painting her toes black. She shows him in by simply stepping back. Her father doesn't stand.

'Mr Harris? Cale Harris?' the man says, extending his hand. It hangs.

Cale Harris continues working. He tucks the rabbit mould into the skin and rolls over the fur like zipping up a sleeping bag. The man wraps his handshake around his folder full of forms.

'I'm here from Moss and Sons. We wrote to you recently regarding an offer on your land. I'm not sure if you received our letter . . . '

'We got it,' Cale says. 'Then we got it again.'

Clary flops onto the foamy seating area of the trailer, one leg dangling, one foot on the ground. She watches the shirt guy look around for something to butter up her father like toast. 'Nice place you have here, really cosy . . . ' Something. He looks at the girl, then back at the dead rabbit.

'Then, you'll know we've made you a very generous offer on your land,' shirt guy says.

'I know,' says Cale.

'We understand drainage is poor and it would take considerable resources to correct. You haven't built on it?'

'Nope.'

'And nor did your father?'

Here it comes again, the offer, the argument. Clary clinks through the jar of glass eyes on the coffee table and lies back, balancing fox eyes on her eyelids. The glass is cold. The jar mists under her fingertips. She balances the eyes on her face, then replaces them with the deer eyes so much bigger than her own. On her back, she pictures living in a supermarket, the trailer smack bang in the middle of the hot-sauce aisle. Shoppers mentally scrape past with shopping carts and peer through the windows to see what's on offer: just a girl and her dad watching *Shark Tank* every night.

Clary removes the deer eyes from her eyelids and gazes into their amber mirrors in her hands. Deer eyes would be cool.

Coffee freckles the papers under the jar, a grain here, a grain there, sprinkled each day. There are more papers somewhere, buried in the forest of the trailer. Clary's surrounded. There's a deer in the bathroom, a crow perches on the closet about to swoop onto bits of cotton wool on the carpet like carrion. Glass eyes watch Clary eat, sleep and pick her nose all day. The hunting store in town used to buy the animals, the museum too. Since the store closed and the museum got computers, business isn't what it was. Clary feels the animals are breeding, crowding in. Yet still her father can't pass anything on a roadside without stopping and wondering if he can make it work.

'Good find today,' he says, swinging a dead raccoon through the door by the tail.

Clary sighs, stroking the rabbit squatted by the kettle, the nook of fur between its ears. Not an antler in sight. There hasn't been a jackalope in years.

There were rules about jackalopes, Clary's father explained. It was Mom's job to hunt them. You could only hunt at night. Jackalopes were skittish, wily and rare as turkey's teeth.

'Is that why I've never seen one hopping around?' Clary used to ask, yawning as he made up her bed. 'Is that where Mom goes all the time?'

Her father placed a finger on his nose: 'Bingo.' He sniffed. The air lingered, clouded with perfume. He stared at the dust framing the absence of a bottle on the shelf, swiped his eyes with the back of his hand and tucked Clary in.

'Let me tell you about jackalopes,' he said. 'On a full moon, you might see one, if you're lucky. You have to be really something to catch them. You have to cover up your scent so they don't sniff you coming. And you have to set a whisky trap so they're easier to catch. Then, you wait. Sometimes you have to wait a long time.'

Clary paints her toenails blue with a bottle of varnish she found on top of the mailbox. The light outside is fading. The sun slots down between the silver trailers like a coin in a machine. Clary's stomach rumbles, followed by her father's. One, then the other, they rumble like drums going to war. It's time.

'You ready?' Cale asks.

Clary scrapes her hair into a cap and grabs her sneakers. The insides stick to her wet toes. They look both ways behind the Megamarket. Cale opens the dumpster.

'One. Two. Three. Umphh.'

He hoists Clary onto his shoulders like a kid at the circus. She dangles into the trash, diving for boxes and glistening Saran Wrap. She claws, tossing packets onto the asphalt. Meat wrapped in slick plastic. Bananas, potatoes, and eggs she must hold carefully while scrambling down.

'Hell yeah,' Cale says, tossing sell-by dates into a duffel bag. 'Why do they need another market? The one they've got don't even sell all they have.'

*

In the trailer's kitchen, everything is more than it looks. The dining table folds down into a bed. The drawer of one cupboard can become a counter; the door of another is secretly an ironing board. And trash can be dinner, and dinner can be victory just like that. Clary puts the eggs in water and watches some sink to the bottom, and some waver, deciding whether to bounce.

'Good eggs,' Cale says. 'Perfectly fine steak. Past its best my . . . '

The room sizzles, smoke off the hotplate hisses into her ears faster than rumours. Clary chews her food slow as a thought. Her father wolfs down the meat, clearing the plate to the dots under the glaze.

'Tastes like fu . . . f . . . fudge you, Mr Megamarket,' he says. 'Oops, sorry pumpkin, not a word you should hear. Don't be cussing at school, pay attention, you don't wanna end up like me.'

Clary laughs, she can't help it. He slips into talking to her like she's six a zillion times a day. His mouth is full of fudge, fluff, sugars and shoots, every word tamed so it won't bite her ears. Yet he's forever apologising, sorry for what he's thinking, rather than what he lets himself say. Clary remembers him arguing with a neighbour when she was small. He reddened like Christmas and clenched his fists.

'You, you . . . ' he said. He spotted her beside him, a child fingering a flower into the dirt. Only muddyfunster would come out of his mouth. The neighbour laughed in his face.

'Let's go,' he'd said.

There were holes under her armpits to sew for school. The cotton blouse in his hands looked slippier to get to grips with than the squirrel he was fixing on the bench. Clary saw him measure every squirrelly inch. Her spine tingled, afraid, as the squirrel got lost, then became itself again. Cale stitched her blouse to the leg of his jeans and said fuck – 'Sorry pumpkin, not a word you should use. Ok?' he said. The girl nodded. She has always understood some words are wood wool, stuffed into gaps to fill holes, and others are flesh, stomachs and hearts. They must be removed.

The trailer is hazed with burnt fat. Clary's father steps out for a cigarette. He looks out to the field. The lights of the trailers are scattered white as litter. Clary flicks nail varnish off her fingers and watches her father consider his land. And again, she pictures the market, right here, a *Buy One, Get One Free* sign above his head. She follows him across the long grass with the petition in her hand, water seeping into her sneakers that blow bubbles at the marsh.

'They can't take away people's homes,' Cale says.

Clary isn't sure. There are fewer trailers than this time last year. Her toes nudge empty cans, Wild Turkey bottles, tread softly around diapers dumped on the grass. It looks less like home than like a pullout on the way.

Outside the steel trailer, a man and a woman sit on deck-chairs, sticks loaded with sausages pointing at a fire.

'How you doing?' says Cale, holding his pen. 'I'm putting together another petition. They can't do nothing if we all stand together.'

The woman glances at her husband. Her husband inspects his sneakers. Cale's pen glints in the firelight. The metal trailer is a flickering mirror of them all.

'That guy was over here today,' the woman says.

'Oh yeah?' says Cale.

'Promised to relocate us, all of us, to that new park outside of town. Hear they have a hot tub, communal laundry, the works.'

The paper crumples in Cale's hand. He turns away, tossing, 'Enjoy your ba– . . . basket sausages,' over his shoulder.

'Come on, Cale! No need to be that way,' the man says. 'Sit, take a load off. Have a beer. Come on! It ain't a bad offer, you could do worse.'

'They just gonna do it anyway,' the woman yells after him.

The words bounce off Cale's back. He walks. Clary does a foxtrot to keep up.

'We could knock on other doors,' she says, one foot on the porch, one inside home. She will go inside if he says, or she will grab the pen and hammer on every door for twenty miles.

'Guess people like hot tubs more than loyalty,' her father says.

Clary knows what he's thinking as he sits on the steps outside. He looks out at the lights over the highway like a poor man's Vegas. His head is full of the help he has given his neighbours, the handout to Mrs Jones when her husband stepped out, Clary's old clothes donated to the Stephensons and their expanding tribe of blonde girls. He can give them cold morning tow-starts till hell freezes over, but they can't give him a signature – won't. He has said these things a hundred times, but tonight, he says nothing. Clary sits beside him, fresh out of what to say. His silence sticks to her thick as the night air. She wishes he would talk. He doesn't even mention the jackalope trail.

The first time a letter came, Cale paced round the trailer. The paper in his fist was fuel on a fire.

'What's it say?' Clary asked.

'Don't worry, pumpkin, someone just wants to buy our land. It won't happen. I won't let it,' he said.

'Where will the jackalopes live?' she said.

That was it. She was a genius, he said. He knew how to make folk sign his petition. He picked up a pen, handed Clary a pad of paper and sat beside her as she wrote the letter.

Deer Everyone,

My name is Clary and I am six years old. I live with my father on a jackalope reserve. Most people don't know it, but jackalopes are rabbits with antlers and they are very VERY rare. Pleese don't take away their home.

Clary's printed letter was sticky-taped to the door. The letters were pouring in, Cale said. Some woman who thought his daughter sounded adorable wanted to sign his petition, so did some guy who hated stores, and someone who had chained herself to diggers seven times. One even arrived from a magazine called *Mysteries*. They wanted to take photos of Clary and Cale wearing deerstalkers on their 'jackalope reserve'. People were on their side, Cale said. Weird people, but people nonetheless.

'Maybe I should start a jackalope trail,' he laughed, after the photographer left. 'People want to believe in all sorts of sh– . . . sherbet.'

He photocopied flyers and left them in the hunting store. Two college kids with skinny cigarettes stopped by.

*

The padlock glares on the dumpster now. Clary and her father stand in the alley like people in a restaurant presented with a dish they don't know how to eat.

'Who locks their trash?' Cale asks.

The air nips Clary's hands. Winter is around the corner, watching their every move with its silvery eye. Her yellow shorts are stuffed in a bag above the water heater. She has dragged out the coat that makes her arms look like Frankenstein.

'What now?' she says.

Cale rakes through his pockets: lighter, keys and loose change. Not enough for a dog or a slice, not enough to be able to say 'shoot' and go home.

'There's other markets,' he says. 'There always is.'

They trail along the highway, cars whipping by. Thirteen-year-old girls lean out the window of a pink limousine and cheer. Clary looks straight ahead at the lights of the Saver store like a beacon. Behind it, the dumpster is open. Pickings are slim. No meat, just eggs, avocados and dill pickles. It will do.

Clary mashes avocado and slices dills into a bowl. The omelette is good. They splash an island of hot sauce next to a swamp of avocado on the plate.

'What's this one called?' her father says.

Clary thinks. It's her job to name every dish, on

days when their haul isn't amazing. The omelette is sandy-coloured and frazzled at the edges. The makeshift guacamole looks like something squished.

'The great Mexican frog rebellion,' she says, dipping egg into green and red.

He has to laugh, wherever he can.

Clary washes the plates. Her father looks an army of stuffed mice in the eye. They stand on the table, some on their tiptoes, some looking down. He groups a few together as if they are friends, angling them just right.

'What do you think?' he says.

Clary looks at the scene. The choir of mice have red jackets and scarves looped around their necks. One wears wire spectacles. One is holding a scrap of paper with squiggles on, all have open mouths like they are ready to sing a mouse song.

'They need something,' Clary says. 'A wool hat with a pompom on top, something like that?'

Cale shrouds two mice wielding polystyrene snowballs in tissue. He sighs, picking up a fat mouse in an apron, positioning the doll's bowl and spoon in her paws.

'Humiliating,' he says, placing it in a box.

Clary stacks the little boxes inside a bigger box by the door and thinks about the black boxes outside.

Humane traps, they're called. The floors are sticky with glue. Once anything is inside it can't get out.

It's early when Cale loads the pick-up. There is nothing in the flat back that looks ready to swoop, bite or run for its life, just mice, messed about with, given people-like poses. He covers the boxes with a tarp and Clary hops in. The radio crackles to another station as they drive into the next town.

'Adorable,' the store owner says. 'We can take more in a few weeks.'

She sits behind the counter, tucking instructions into plastic packets of worry dolls. Cale stares at the stick people, legs and arms bound with colourful string. Little squares of paper litter the counter. *Place a worry doll under your pillow each night, tell her your problems and when you wake they'll have disappeared.*

The shop owner looks at Cale and leans forward with worry dolls in her hand.

'You want some?' she says.

Cale steps back, the way he does when women are too nice and smile for no reason. He looks around for Clary. She is wandering around the store inspecting displays of kitchen whisks shaped like rabbit ears, lamps shaped like bears, candles that look like fancy slices of cake. Everything is shaped like something it isn't. Cale shakes his head at the worry dolls in the shopkeeper's hand.

'So you're making another order?' he asks.

'Sure,' the woman says, stroking a mouse ear with her fingertip. 'Can you do some mice on bicycles?'

'Where the fu– . . . flip am I going to get a little mouse bicycle?'

'I think it's called a micycle, Dad,' Clary says, standing behind him.

The woman laughs. 'I don't know. Maybe a skateboard? Or a skiing mouse then?'

Clary pictures another trip to the doll store, a mouse in her father's pocket, everything held close for size. He puts his hands in his flannel pockets and walks to the door without looking back. The woman watches him go, stroking her ponytail like a pet. Outside, two teenage girls approach the store saying, 'We got to go in here! This store has some cool weird crap.'

'That's a weird fucking store,' Clary says. 'Who spends all their money on candles that look like cakes? They all melt the same.'

'Damned if I know what people spend their money on, pumpkin,' Cale says. 'Damn, pumpkin, what have I told you about cussing?'

Clary grins, pretty sure she'll be a pumpkin her whole fucking life.

*

The mice on the table are no longer carollers. One sniffs a flower, two hold paws. Clary fiddles with a mouse with nothing in its paws. Ideally, it would clutch a box of chocolates, or be proffering a teensy jewellery box, but there aren't any small enough in the doll's house store. Cale opens the letter and runs his hand over his head to wipe the crease off his brow.

'The landowners either side of us sold,' he says.

Clary reads the letter, then studies his face, unable to determine what it means.

'If they wanted, they could build around us,' she says. 'Smaller stores, or something.'

The shirt guy reminded them of this when he stopped by again. His jacket was fastened, no handshake was offered, slices of paper left his hand.

'Obviously, that wouldn't be the most advantageous solution,' he said, 'but . . . '

Advantageous, Clary thought. She wasn't sure how to spell it. It sounded like outrageous with advantages tagged on.

Cale straps the last box into the pick-up. Clary winds down the window, lets the cold air hit her all the way out of town. There are hearts in the store window, shiny foil-covered chocolate hearts, heart-shaped cushions, a speckling of cuddly toys with *I Love You* stitched to their chests like tattoos.

'Hey!' The woman behind the counter grins as if she's bumped into an old friend, but it's just Cale delivering more mice. His daughter trails behind him, looking at everything on the shelves. He hands over the box of new mice. The woman says 'awww', opens the till and counts notes into his hand one at a time, her finger like a fortune-teller's on his palm.

'The last mice sold out in a week,' she says. 'Can you mount anything else? Nothing too big. Something sweet. I'd *love* something for Easter.'

She looks at Cale with something in her voice bigger than a mouse. Cale looks at her bare finger stroking a tail and looks away.

'Dunno,' he says.

Clary is behind him, right there, like his manager, like all her looking at the weird stuff nearby was a ruse and she was waiting to jump in and do what she had to do.

'Of course he can do something else,' she says. 'He can do anything.'

'Great, swing by some time and show me what you've got,' the woman says.

They are silent all the drive home, Clary and Cale. She knows he is still thinking about the letter. They look out the windows at the low sun, pools of snow preserved in the shadows of buildings the sunlight can't touch. They don't speak until they're back at the trailer, eating a pizza they bought on the way home.

'Maybe we should sell,' Clary says. She does not want to say it, she thought she never would, but she does. She says it like a curse word something won't let her censor. Her father chews pizza, staring at the letter on the table, a string of cheese connecting the slice to his lips.

'That's no way to think, pumpkin, giving up. It's our land. Besides, where will the jackalopes live?'

He grins best he can, his lips not connected to his eyes.

'There aren't any jackalopes, Dad,' says Clary. 'Mom only ever hunted dickalope.'

She looks at him, waiting to be corrected for her language, unsure if she'll ever be a pumpkin again. Cale puts down his slice. The silence stretches between them like cheese on that pizza, thinning, fit to snap.

'If we aren't here, how can she come back?' he says.

Clary looks around the trailer, thinking about her mother. Their life seemed to fit her like the skin of a rabbit on a hare. She was bigger than it. Clary opens her mouth, unable to make her voice low enough for her not to be able to hear it. It's just words, laid out like red-hot sauce, or thread, on the counter.

'She's never coming back,' she says.

*

Clary chooses the antlers for the jackalope. Cale lets her watch him work on the rabbit. She squishes the clay that holds in the eyes and watches it transform into something beyond itself. Finally, it's ready. The rabbit's antlers rut the spring air like hooks, ready to hang someone's keys on. Clary puts it in the box and they drive. Together, they stand at the counter of the store. Cale sets the box down. The woman at the till peers inside the box, removing a mist of tissue paper snared on an antler.

'I made this. I can do as many as you like,' Cale says. 'If you wanna give it a go?'

CATWOMAN HAD SOMETHING

My mother's sister was almost Catwoman. Once, she showed me her kitty ears and a pointy little mask she wore for a Spandex audition in the sixties. It was down to her and one other woman, she said. She was floating off to Key West with some guy she met at the store and missed their call. Since then, she'd had eight lives – whiskers of them included us. She didn't need more. She had something, she had *it*, a wow no one could put their finger on.

Strictly, Judy wasn't my aunt, more of a fraction of an aunt, a slither. She was Mom's half-sister, the bad half or the good, depending on how you feel. They didn't meet until Mom was nineteen. Mom stood with a red carnation in her hat. Judy stepped off the train in crocodile shoes, a waft of perfume and a dizzying laugh. Later, Mom had to tell me it all in slow motion. The man in the raincoat propping up a weepy girlfriend looked over her shoulder. The conductor loosened his grip on a ticket-dodging kid and watched Judy slink past. She only had eyes for red carnations.

The women stared at each other like a before and after on a makeover show. Mom looked at Judy and saw her future, if she was a different sort of girl. And Judy saw what she could have been like when she was young, if she'd never learned to walk in heels. Walking right is something 'a girl shouldn't learn till she's twenty-one', Judy said. Mom never got the hang of it, so she married a surveyor.

I was nothing like either of them. I wanted to be Cat-woman, but my posture sucked. I didn't think I'd ever be someone who always wears heels – what happens when you have to run?

Every Christmas I sent Judy cards of snowmen and nativity scenes with kitty ears and masks drawn on in magic marker. She sent us postcards of red buses and monkeys in temples. She was part of our family like a cat who comes and goes, but mostly goes. We left a hole in the door all the same.

When my grandfather died, Judy returned from what Mom called 'swanning about'. Her pale hands fluttered over her black dress with white ribbon on the trim. The inside of her purse winked at me, a glint of satin, pink as a kitten's mouth. Cosmetics sparkled like foil-wrapped candies.

'Do you want some?' she said, offering lipstick.

I took off the cap, stared at the bullet of the tip.

'Judy, what are you thinking? She's only *seven*,' Mom

said. She glared as if red was tattooed to my mouth. 'Lana, go scrub your face!'

I smeared my glamorous mouth into the Joker in the mirror.

'There's no harm in it,' Judy said. 'Shouldn't us girls look our best for Dad one last time?'

Nothing bothered her: worry belonged to a whole other species of women who didn't paint their nails. They'd both known different fathers, I think. Judy's was a man with a sandy quiff and a wink, popping to a bar to sell electrical appliances without a warranty, and not popping back when she was ten. Mom's father was older. He huddled in a retirement village. Women waved Mom over in aprons they wore to make packet soup or watch *The Price is Right*. They were inconsolable.

'Your dad's chucked me,' an English lady called Pisky said.

Mom wasn't sure what to say. Later, she told me my grandfather was no longer going to the seventy-four-year-old woman's house for tea. He'd switched to mango juice and pruning the little ball-shaped trees outside the door of a woman of seventy-two.

I was listening to it all, figuring things out. Judy, me and Mom had the same eyes, but Judy's were cat's eyes on a highway. Mom's were quiet as lamps that aren't plugged in. Everyone said Judy was like her father, while Mom took after her mom. Who I was wasn't clear. 'She's so like her mother!' they said, when I organised my dolls by hair colour on the shelf. 'She's just like Judy!' they said, when I laughed in the wrong place or refused to wear nylon because I got scratchy. I didn't like how people said it. It was like they were squeezing me into a hand-me-down leather suit, tattooing on a cat mask I'd be stuck with for ever, even if I became a dentist. I fought it, doing my best not to be Mom or Catwoman, and just be me. Whatever that was.

For a while, that was some sort of GI Jane. Studying for my exams, I wore boots and combat pants like a get-out clause. I walked and Judy winced. Mom frowned at the sound of me, like the Hulk clunking downstairs for coffee and muffins. I wasn't ladylike, they agreed, whatever that means. For Mom, ladylike was running water into the sink so no one would ever hear her go to the bathroom. For Judy, it was wiggles and frills. Even when she had to walk with a cane she wrapped the handle in lace and wore satin gloves so no one saw the veins in her hands stand to attention as she leaned on the stick. Another thing in her ladylike package was her laugh. That husky purr. Even as an ageing woman, if you heard her, you'd turn around expecting to see a girl practising for the sexiest laugh contest. Mom didn't approve.

'Is it really suitable for a woman your age?' she said, as Judy bypassed the thermals in the outlet store for the silk camisoles. None of us were sure how old she really was. (Judy said 'a lady never reveals her bust size or her age'.)

'If you don't *feel* like a lady in your underwear, how can you expect to *act* like one?' she said to the underpants in the packet.

Mom came back alone to buy a plaid bathrobe for Judy's birthday. We found it over the canary's cage with instructions to sit the cage by the window and let the bird fly once a day. Judy had flitted off again, migrated to Spain with a man who had a theory it was cheaper than heating his house in Colorado all winter.

Mom often said it was a pity Judy never found 'the one' and settled down. She had to: she married a man who began most of his sentences with 'actually . . . ' I don't think Judy felt she missed out. I only heard her mention marriage once. She'd been seeing some widower for a while. Mom was doing backflips.

'Do you think you'll get married?'

Judy's laugh meowed as if she'd caught her tail in a mousetrap.

'Married? If you love cake would you want only Twinkies for thirty years?'

I started thinking of red velvet cake, baked Alaska, whoopie pie . . .

Catwoman had something, a secret that didn't make marriage necessary. No one could figure out how, even on her eighth life, Judy always had boyfriends. That's what she called them, boyfriends. We'd stop by her apartment to find her pouring coffee, old men blushing, laughing, like being a boyfriend flushed the years away. I'd never called anyone a boyfriend myself. Once, when I was seven, I punched this boy in the face, POW! He showed up at my door the next day, asking me to play.

'She's so like Judy,' Dad said.

'Go away. You smell like candy apples,' I said, slamming the door in the boy's face. I can't remember his name, but I remember his smell, sticky sweet, like if I licked him I'd get toothache.

In my senior year, I got married, at least mentally, to a boy in my class called Noah. I wasn't Catwoman. I didn't go on dates. Noah and I only spoke in English, and not to each other. We spoke via *Much Ado*, *The Great Gatsby*, one comment laid on top of the other, agreeing, sparring, intertwined. His cold-looking hands fidgeted under a gangly jumper. I looked at him and promised to see him, only him, when I saw movies. I was Superman; he was Lois Lane. He was Rhett Butler, I was Scarlett. I promised to impose only Noah's face onto every movie kiss and advert.

I doubted Catwoman ever felt such devotion. Judy hopped from one boyfriend to another. She found them all over, even where people only talk to say they have the wrong change or don't need a bag – supermarkets, petrol stations, restaurants, the timber place Mom called when the fence wanted fixing.

'How much did you pay for it?' Judy asked.

Mom told her. Judy shook her head. 'I could have got it cheaper,' she said.

Whatever Mom bought, her sister said she could have got it cheaper with her 'blonde discount' – the bathroom sink from the plumbing place, shingles for the shed. Mom refused to take her to the builders' yard EVER again. Every time Judy giggled, twining her smile around the guy behind the counter like a silky tail on a leg. She always got things at cost.

'It's embarrassing on a woman her age. There'll come a day when that discount of hers will run out,' Mom said.

It didn't. Catwoman's lives ran out just in time, and her secret was mine.

On the Saturday before she died, Judy sat by the window like she was soaking the sunlight into her skin for later. She invited me around for tea, just me. It was unusual enough to seem important, like she was going to leap off the rooftop and show me she really had been Catwoman all along, but when I got there she just poured Earl Grey, feathers on the cuff of her cardigan dipping into her china cup. I sipped, wondering how long I should stay. I liked

Judy, but if I liked her too much Mom would think we were forming some sort of gang against her.

'So, you're not courting?' said Judy.

'No, I haven't time.' I was glad of study. Books were camouflage for a girl who didn't know how to stand out.

Judy nodded, like she heard beyond words. The red in my cheeks ratted me out.

'I have something for you, if anything ever happens to me: an inheritance. It's for you. Only.'

'Don't be stupid! Nothing's going to happen,' I said.

My laughter wafted over the fact she was getting on, and '*if* anything happens' meant when.

Judy would have loved her funeral if it hadn't been, you know, her funeral, and Mom hadn't picked out her clothes. Mom insisted on a suit jacket and blouse buttoned to the neck, like Judy might have some sort of interview at the pearly gates and these clothes could stop her getting fresh with St Peter. I thought we should let Judy wear the kitty ears and cat mask, but Mom said it was too sad, to be dressed forevermore as someone she almost was.

There were men outside the church just shuffling around with no one to laugh at their jokes or ask interesting questions about the responsibilities their jobs must entail. Who these men were, we had no idea. Mom said Judy always landed on her feet, except the day she fell down the stairs. No matter what, she always landed herself a man. And here they were, jammed into a room with silk flowers after the service. I'd never seen so many stages of frowns on middle-aged men. Their whole faces looked like they'd never recover from the downturn.

'Incredible woman,' one man said to another. It sounded like it had a capital I and W like a superhero: the Incredible Woman, thwarting bad guys with her laugh, the toss of her hair like a cape.

'Amazing,' said the man opposite him.

The men didn't look each other in the eye, two strangers raising a toast to a woman who, I supposed, both had shared their beds with.

Later, I heard one man say 'catnip'.

'First time I met Juju, I didn't think she was that pretty, you know, no prettier than any other woman – but she had something about her, like catnip,' he said. 'I couldn't keep away.'

'Who could?' the other man said. 'To catnip.'

Chink chink. Two raised glasses met.

We drove to Judy's apartment later to clear out her stuff and claim my inheritance. I pictured a boatload of stolen cash wrapped in red ribbon, a velvet pouch full of diamonds and a signed confession she'd been a spy. 'Inheritance' sounded like a big deal: formal, important. Judy told me like she had some sort of cat sense she was dying, though she couldn't have. It was sudden, she slipped on a juice box outside. There was a note taped to an ottoman in the bedroom.

Lana's Inheritance, it said.

'Inheritance!' Mom said. 'Would you get a load of that!'

The stuff Mom once said about her sister with a sigh now had exclamation marks and a smile, happier in the past tense. She opened Judy's wardrobe and slung clothes in a sack. I opened the ottoman, filled to the brim with oil paintings, the real Mona Lisa . . . who knew that? It was full of perfume, that's it: all identical, dozens of old-fashioned glass bottles Judy would have said held 'cologne'. I opened a cap and sniffed. The perfume didn't smell like much, not romance or moonlight, or some girl chasing a balloon in Paris like adverts wanted me to believe. It wasn't spicy or flowery or anything in particular, but inhaling it I remembered Judy instantly, so vividly I could have been on a train with her on the way to the zoo, ice cream on my fingers washed with her handkerchief and spit. I closed the lid and stashed the bottles in the closet in my room when I got home. I didn't know what to do with them, but I felt like an ass throwing away anything called an inheritance.

*

It was almost Christmas when I considered the perfume again. There was a costume party. Everyone had to go as a dead poet. I hadn't a clue who to be. I clawed through boxes of clothes in the attic, raking up what Judy wore when she was young: a cat mask, miniskirts, circle dresses, cottony prints that believed life was as simple as daisies. It seemed like a start – the clothes had the look of a more lyrical time. I hung the dresses on the hook on my door and was overcome by the scent – a draught of my aunt wafted into the room. I missed her, suddenly, so hard I had to sit down.

I put on a dress I couldn't imagine Catwoman in. It was covered in poppies, rippling like a field. I walked into the party alone. It was just like I thought – random. There were a few Allen Ginsbergs covering zits with fake beards. There was a guy in lederhosen for no reason I could name. The girls took it more seriously: poetry books poked out their purses, but other than what the jackets said it was impossible to tell who they were. Amazingly, one girl spoke to me. Stephanie. She walked over in a black flapper dress, beads jittering.

'Razors pain you . . . ' she said. 'I love your costume, it suits you.'

I shrugged, not really anyone (at a push I'd say Anne Sexton or Plath).

Stephanie smiled, hanging, like she wanted to say more but didn't know what.

'Who do you think I am?' a tall Ginsberg interrupted.

'I have no idea.'

'How about me?' Another Ginsberg, a short one, was at my side. Then another. Then a kid in a sheepy sweater I think wanted to be Ted Hughes. They were all offering me drinks and desperate to hear my opinion of who I thought they were. I thought about Judy, her giggle squeezing through a crowd. Is this what she felt like? I was having a hard time not laughing myself. I looked through the poets. The boy from English was dressed in pyjamas and a hunter hat. Kurt Cobain/Noah watched me from across the room.

It wasn't Catwoman who looked back at me in the mirror in my bathroom. I didn't have a giggle or a purr, more of a snicker muffled by one hand. Yet, something was different. I looked the same, but guys who never usually spoke to me all wanted to give me a ride home. On Monday, I paid attention to my clothes. I couldn't wait for Noah to look at me like Kurt Cobain again. He was in the library, so were a couple of Ginsbergs from the party – except now they just had names like Aidan or Chris. I browsed the shelves. Noah looked up, and turned back to his book. No one else even glanced.

The poppy dress swayed on the back of the door, not smelling of ice cream, daytrips or Judy, just detergent.

There was a flatness in my stomach, the feeling I had at the party ironed out. Catwoman never had this problem; men saw her and purred her name in her ear. I sat in my room thinking about Judy, wishing I knew her secret. I took out a bottle of her perfume and dabbed it on my wrists before I went to the Korean for snacks.

The shopkeeper watched me like I might slip something in my pocket.

'Anything else?' he said.

'No.'

'Are you sure? Look . . . '

He came around the counter to show me the vegan stuff he'd just started stocking, the soy milk and herbs. He kept talking, grabbing things off the shelves, showing me like he couldn't let me leave before I approved.

I dabbed on the scent the next morning. Noah pulled out my chair in the canteen, a few of the guys from the party watched. Some guy called Chris stopped by our table to invite me to a party, the others smiled over, all eyes. Judy would have approved.

'I'm sorry, I'm busy, maybe next time,' I told Chris. I laughed for no reason, it fizzed out of me like shaken cola. I was fizzing from everyone looking at me so hard. It was a rush.

*

Noah pulled his sleeves over his dermatitis. The museum was a birdcage of a building full of crawling and still things, wood-boring bees under glass and stuffed animals behind velvet ropes: dead foxes, perched crows, a lion with bullet holes in its back. We looked at sad holes in the lion's flank. Noah took a Band-Aid out his pocket, crossed the velvet rope and stuck it on the stuffed animal's wounds. I kissed him. Who wouldn't? He tasted milky sweet like rice pudding. We left holding hands.

It was raining. Walk/Don't Walk smeared orange light on the wet street like jelly. We crossed to a café and sat behind some college guys. They all looked sort of the same: handsome and sure and clean. They looked at me and huddled. One came over. I wasn't good at this, navigating how to be polite to some guy while still making the one beside me feel like no one else existed. WWJD – What Would Judy Do?

'Sounds like a cool party, I'll see if I can make it,' I laughed. Where did it come from? I was one of those girls, laughing all over the place. I couldn't keep it in. Noah fidgeted with his sleeves and went to the restroom. He came back to find some guy sat in his seat talking, talking, as I laughed and laughed. Noah hovered at the counter, unsure how to come back. I wanted to stand up and go over, but I didn't. The college guy was looking at me so much, listening to everything I said.

'I've got a surprise for you,' Noah said outside.

He rolled up his sleeve to show me L A N A, my name scratched into his arm, bloody, indelible, a series of cat scratches. I didn't know what to say. Why did he do that? We stood outside the café, college guys pressed to the window breathing on the glass, drawing hearts in their breath. One drew a penis. I laughed. Noah rolled down his sleeve.

'Call me when you get home?' he said.

In the reflection of the café window I saw myself smile vaguely, random guys and Noah all looking. I wanted to kiss him, lay my hand on his red scars, something, but I didn't, I was just looking. It felt like a weight, everyone looking for something from me to make their day. How did Catwoman manage it? I couldn't recall Judy ever looking troubled. Sad stuff happened and she sat by the window, closed her eyes and let the sun bounce off her, Catwoman to the bone. I didn't think I could ever be like that. Noah looked so sad, lost. I imagined my name scarring him all his life, something to be explained to whomever he married, doctors, swimmers, holiday-goers, coroners, next of kin. I was an identifying mark. I'll throw away the perfume when I get home, I decided. I visualised unscrewing silver lids, pouring bottle after bottle down the toilet, flushing it into the ocean to make irresistible fish or something.

'Later,' I said, walking towards Mom's car pulling in on the corner.

I turned around. The college guys were piling out of the café and looking in my direction; so was Noah. I stood a little taller and put on a wiggle so as not to disappoint them. I imagined Catwoman twitching a tail, slinking into the night. It was less than a block to the car, Mom and a trip to the mall – shoes on sale, a shirt to be returned, it was a long walk. I felt those guys watching me, right now, all of them. The image of myself tipping the perfume away disappeared faster than my breath in the cold. I just couldn't see it. Catwoman would get it, maybe no one else does. Their eyes felt like sun on my skin. I felt their eyes on my hips wind my walk into a tick-tock. Who can fight what they inherit? I used it. Sure, there'd be other boys, sad boys, desperate guys, men showing off, scars, bad tattoos; I tried not to think about it. Not yet. I couldn't imagine walking through life knowing no one was watching me walk away.

BOYS LIKE DOLLS

Nathan's GI Joe is his friend, sort of. There's a scar on his cheek he won't talk about. Nathan touches the smooth plastic welt. Joe spits.

'Women love it, son. Don't let anyone tell you a man can't be someone with a scar. Scars are what we are.'

Nathan nods. This is exactly the sort of thing Joe always says.

When the doll first spoke, the boy wasn't shocked. He'd arranged Joe's hands to grip onto the cliff of the window-ledge. Eagle eyes looked up, positioned with the lever on the back of Joe's head. Blue sky rushed through the glass. Joe lost his grip and slipped.

'Shit,' he said.

The carpet was beige, dusty and stained. Nathan looked at the doll on the floor, bare feet like paddles pointing out of different sides of a boat. If Joe was a person, the bone would have broken. If he was a person who fell this way, 'shit' is exactly what he'd say.

'Joe?' Nathan said.

'Private,' Joe said. 'What now, Sergeant? Sarge?'

Plastic eyes stared.

'I'm Nathan,' the boy said.

The doll lay down, poseable ankles twisted. His valiant salute to his beret had been lost as soon as he was taken out of the box.

'Private Joe, reporting for duty, Sarge.'

'I'm Nathan,' Nathan said. 'I'm not a sergeant, I don't think.'

'Yes sir!'

Nathan looked at Joe, awaiting orders. He'd never given orders before. No one ever called him 'sir'. (Once, on a birthday card, his aunt wrote *esquire* on the envelope, but it wasn't the same.) Giving orders might be kinda cool; Nathan left Joe to guard sheets of newspaper under his bed.

'Let no one see them,' he said. 'That's an order.'

It was still early. Nathan's mother was in Helen's room, trying to dress his sister between bounces on the bed. Thud. The newspaper dropped through the letterbox. Nathan snuck downstairs with a sheet of newspaper under his arm, just in case. He flicked through the paper. All clear. Today was ok. There were no pages he had to replace with stories about albino hedgehogs or a raccoon out of nowhere messing up someone's lawn.

'Nathaaaaaaaaaaaan.'

On Saturday, Nathan's mother calls upstairs. She makes his name so long he's bored before he's even there. He leaves Joe in the snowy pillow mountains and runs. It's shopping day again.

'Put your shoes on,' Nathan's mother says.

Helen is all ready in the hall, bundled into the lazy-mobile of her buggy, though she's old enough to walk. Nathan buttons his coat.

'Don't forget your scarf,' says his mother.

The scarf is itchy and striped yellow, red and blue. Nathan loops it around around his neck and thinks of Joe calling him Sarge.

The bus is rammed with old ladies with wheelie bags and women with buggies. Everyone gets on the bus to cough, cough, cough, cough. Everything is in the air. Nathan pulls his scarf over his mouth, remembering his mother spraying piney fresh all over the house.

'Chemical warfare,' Joe says. 'Cover your mouth. Quick!'

Nathan's mother rings the bell twice to get off at Quids In. Inside, she picks up a basket and hands another to Nathan. Stroking her chin, she considers tinned vegetables, crisps, packet rice and biscuits close to their *best before*.

'Can I have this, Mum? Can I?' Nathan asks.

He is clutching a piece of cardboard with a desert painted on. Brittle plastic is moulded over a plastic ammunition belt, boots, a helmet and cotton fatigues. Everything rests in perfectly shaped slots like shoes on sand.

'Put it back,' his mother says. She is looking in her purse, counting change, subtracting money for the bus into one compartment and figuring out how many tins of soup she can buy with the rest. There's no chance of a helmet. Helen has grabbed a pair of plastic shoes and a tiara and is waving them around.

'Nathan,' his mother says.

She looks at him with too much in her hands: purse, bag, a box of cereal, the wire handle of the shopping basket hooped over her elbow. It's up to him to wrestle the princess shoes off his sister. He tugs and she wails. He tugs, she wails like the plastic shoes in her hand are on a string connected to her mouth.

'Sshh,' Nathan says. 'Are you going to be a man or a little girl?'

His sister looks at him with an open mouth. Everything about her is pink, from the flowers on her tights to the bow clipped to her hair. Everything screams 'little girl'. Yet, she stares at Nathan and stops whining. Sometimes Joe is a good guy to know.

Nathan's mother pushes the buggy to the checkout. Behind her, he spots his chance. He thinks of Joe's bare feet and rams the soldier clothes into his waistband under his coat. Walking to the counter, he's rigid, the cardboard like a six-pack strapped over his belly and everything fluttering inside. They are halfway out the door. Yes! Home free. Nathan can feel his pulse racing like a car on a plastic track.

'Excuse me . . .'

The shopkeeper holds a price gun in one hand, the other taps Nathan's mother's shoulder. He's not smiling; he looks like he's forgotten how. The boy's mother turns, buggy jamming the doorway. People wait to get past.

'What's this?' the shopkeeper says.

Nathan's heart plummets to his stomach. The shopkeeper holds a silver coin in his mother's face.

'Foreign,' the shopkeeper says. 'You gave me this.'

'Did I? Sorry.'

Blushing, she takes out her purse, gives him the right coins and leaves. Nathan turns in the street, half expecting to be chased.

Wind kicks the leaves in the gutters. Walking through the houses is less windy, Nathan's mother says. She's overspent. They must walk halfway home, then take the bus the rest of the way. Carrier bags dig trenches in

Nathan's palms. Now and then, his mother pauses and says, 'That's a nice front door, isn't it?' or 'I love those windows.' He doesn't understand how anyone can love something like windows. She stops, pulls the hood over the buggy to protect Helen from the drizzle and looks at shiny white windows. Some have the front page of a newspaper taped to the glass. The newspaper is a flag with a photo of a grinning soldier in the centre. There are only three words on it: 'Support Our Troops'. Nathan wonders if the people who put the paper in the window have dads in the service, brothers or sons. The wind blows in his ears; they ache. He sees Spiderman curtains in one window and wishes he could knock on the door and go in; his mother looks as if she is thinking the same and would love to make friends with someone for a while. Maybe there's a kid in the Spiderman house just like him he could talk to, but he can't. Joe wouldn't like him talking to people for a start, his lips are a sealed plastic line.

'Tell no one nothing,' he says. 'You admit your fears and stuff can start to bug you, seem real.'

And nothing is all Nathan tells everyone all day long.

Under raindrops on her clear plastic bubble, Helen is asleep as they arrive home. Nathan stares at the newspaper taped to their window as his mother rummages for keys. The soldier's grin is almost white, bleached by the sun.

'I could have sworn we still had some packets of pasta left,' Nathan's mother says. 'Where does it all go?'

She unpacks the groceries, but he can't help. Stiffly, Nathan walks upstairs, rips into the cardboard packaging under his coat and undresses Joe quickly, not looking at his smooth groin or touching the abs etched into his torso like scars. The jumpsuit is spattered in brown and green splodges that don't camouflage with the carpet or the white flowers on the wallpaper. The helmet fits. Nathan stands the soldier on tiptoes like a ballerina to get his feet in the boots.

'Bit of a squeeze, Sarge,' Joe says.

His toes strain at soft plastic. Nathan squeezes the boot the way his mother decides if he needs new shoes. Tearing the cardboard packaging to bits, he hides it under his bed.

'*Made in Taiwan*,' Joe reads the scrap of card at his feet. 'It figures.'

Nathan knew it would bug him. He doesn't think there's ever been a war with Taiwan, but it doesn't matter to Joe. It's another country.

'Anywhere could be the enemy,' says Joe, 'anyone.'

Nathan looks at the doll handed down by his cousins. Sometimes Nathan wants to argue, but who knows where Joe's been? How many wars he's seen?

*

It's Saturday again. Nathan's mother runs through the hall in rabbit slippers, tripping over foam ears. She barges through Nathan's door with an envelope in her hand. This time it's not a letter from school. She isn't asking him why he wouldn't take off his scarf in class.

'He's coming home!' she says. 'Really, this time.'

'Great,' Nathan says.

He wants to believe her, smile with her, but he can't feel his face. His mouth feels like a foot he's been sitting on too long. The door gapes when she leaves.

'We need shelter, Sarge,' Joe says. 'Somewhere to figure out manoeuvres.'

Nathan builds a fort with a blanket and chairs by the bed. Inside glows orange, the lamp lights up the old blanket, revealing thick and thin patches. It feels quieter in the tent than anywhere in the house, though the walls are just wool. Sometimes, in the tent, Nathan tries to talk.

'What's it like, Joe,' he says, 'where you've been?'

'Sshh,' Joe says. 'Look out.'

Nathan positions Joe's eagle eyes sideways. From his voice, he knows that's what Joe wants. He places a plastic gun in his hand pointing at the door. The end of the gun is slightly chewed from when Nathan was bored. There are lots of chewed things in the room; Nathan chews everything he can get. He likes biting something firm, seeing the size of the dents his teeth can make in things.

He looks at Joe's left thumb now, chewed to the knuckle, the tip spread out like a spatula. He was sorry he chewed it once Joe started to talk.

'I'm sorry about your thumb,' he says again.

Joe's on the look-out, not looking at his thumb.

'Can't feel it,' he says.

Joe wakes Nathan up with a hiss: 'Patrol,' he says. Nathan can hear birds. He gets up, listening, and stands in the hallway guarding the letterbox, ready. The newspaper pushes through into his hand. On his knees, Nathan flicks through the paper. There's a picture inside of a flag over a box and people with brass stars on their hats standing still. He scrunches it into a ball in his pocket.

'Is that the paper?' his mother says.

She walks towards him with a mug of tea in her hand. There isn't time to replace the page with a story about fish with bellies that look like smiling faces. He watches her read over cornflakes. When she comes to the missing sheet she frowns.

'There's a page missing,' she says. 'Again. I think that paperboy's stealing them for the comic strips or something.' She looks out of the window, picturing a boy on a bike collecting crosswords or page threes, stashing them under his bed. Nathan's heart pounds.

'Maybe he just dropped them,' he says.

She shrugs, flipping the page. Everything is ok, what's missing is skimmed. The sort of page that makes her look at the letter again isn't there. 'I hope they actually let him come home this time.'

It's almost bonfire night. Outside, fireworks whoop and whine. Nathan's mother cleans out closets, tossing old shoes into a pile.

'Lie low!' Joe says.

Nathan slides on his belly in the tent. The streetlights are on outside, though it should still be day. Joe's stomach grumbles on time.

'Mess time,' Joe says.

Nathan opens a packet of rice and holds grains to Joe's lips. They won't open. His plastic stomach is hollow, but every day it rumbles, regular as the chiming clock in Nathan's grandmother's lounge. Nathan holds the food close to Joe's nose, hoping he can smell it and will go back on duty full, not realising he didn't really eat.

'How we doing for rations, Sarge?' Joe asks.

Rations are low. There are packets of rice under the bed, but Joe won't 'eat' from one that's already open: 'How do we know it's not contaminated, Sarge?'

Nathan waits till his mother stops moving around. It takes time. Even when she does stop, she doesn't really. In the middle of game shows, she says, 'The skirting in the hall needs painting. I'll do it tomorrow.' Everything in the house stands on parade. Helen needs new sparkly tights. Nathan must have new laces in his shoes. Finally, she is still. Nathan listens to her in the lounge, a pretty woman is falling in love through the walls. He looks both ways and creeps into the kitchen with bare feet. He knows how far to open a door before it squeals. Stuffing packets of pasta in his jeans, he moves along. In the cupboard by the mugs is the stuff his mother stashes like a squirrel for special occasions. He takes a bottle of whisky, pours some into his Superman flask, tops up the bottle with water and puts it back.

Upstairs, boy and doll lie with their eyes open. Joe doesn't sleep in the bed, he's not that sort of doll. His close-cropped hair is like Velcro. Everything sticks, stray feathers and lint. Nathan hears him under the bed, sock pulled over his chest like a sleeping bag, murmuring in the dark.

The boy and soldier listen. They've been listening for weeks. Their days in the tent are numbered. They know it. Joe's eyes are shiny, but then, they always are. The vacuum cleaner bashes skirting boards behind the walls. The bedroom door opens and the walls of their world tremble, the vacuum cleaner at the sides. Knelt in sniper mode at the entrance of the tent, Joe is knocked to the floor by the flex. He lies in deafening darkness, head sucked into the hose. Everything goes quiet with a click. Nathan's mother peers into the tent.

'You need to take this down, Nathan, so I can hoover,' she says. Pulling the blockage of Joe's head out of the tube, she tosses him down. 'You're old enough to tidy your own room.'

Nathan takes down the tent as Joe watches from the ground.

'I'm not gonna make it, Sarge,' he says.

Nathan hides their rations under his bed. The vacuum cleaner is getting close again, so he sits Joe on the shelf.

'Sarge, you can't leave me like this. I need help.'

'Aren't you supposed to say "Go on without me, save yourself" or summat?' says Nathan.

'Fuck that,' says Joe.

Nathan looks at Joe, the same as always, lint on his head. He sounds shaken, like something from an old movie – a cowboy with one red strand trickling from his lips. Nathan gets the whisky, one eye on the door. He pours some onto Joe's face and rips toilet-roll bandages.

'It hurts, Sarge.'

'Where?'

'I don't know.'

Nathan licks a drop of whisky off Joe's chin, tasting fire.

*

It's not easy, leaving Joe for school, but Nathan does. Sharpening his pencil, he thinks 'Where does it hurt?' and still doesn't know. The class are reading out papers about their families. A girl with skin the colour of perfect toast offers around little pastry sweets.

'Just like Jaddati makes,' she says.

She smiles at Nathan. He looks down, fingers sticky from the sweet in his hand. When it's his turn to read, he stutters and skims. He cannot tell the smiling girl they might be enemies. She is wearing pink tights like his sister's, but her grandmother lives in another country. Whose side is she on? He isn't sure.

After school, Nathan's mother scrub-scrubs everything clean one last time. In his bedroom, Nathan can hear knives scraping burnt pans. Joe's voice shivers, his belly is hard. Nathan listens to a stool being dragged across the lino in the kitchen downstairs.

'Someone's been here. Something's not right,' says Joe.

Nathan follows Joe's gaze to the door, his little sister's writing beside it on the wall. *Helen. Helen. Hel.* The writing slopes down then gets bored with itself. Nathan sighs. His sister writes her name everywhere all day long. Sometimes, he thinks he'll go to sleep and wake to find himself covered: *Helen Helen Hel* all over his face. Next to the scrawled wall, one of her dolls is abandoned on the floor. The doll is called Skipper; it looks like a child with a too grown-up face. It lies face-up, staring at glow-in-the-dark stars stuck to a white ceiling. The stars aren't glowing now. Joe can't look away.

'Close my eyes,' Joe says.

Nathan tries the switch at the back of Joe's skull. Blue eyes move side to side. There's nothing to make them close.

'I can't close them,' Nathan says.

'Why?'

Joe's voice is a splinter. He can't stop staring at Skipper lying on the ground.

'Who did that?' he says. 'I didn't do it. Walking through the village, I saw two local children and gave them chocolate. Walking back, they were lying down, the wrapper still in their hands. I saw the "thank you" still in the girl's throat. Cut. Open like a red flower.'

Nathan looks at the doll on the floor, still just a doll, light dabbed to its eye. He holds Joe in his hands. Joe can't stop seeing, even facing the window, the yellow weeds on next door's wall waving in the wind.

'What's that stain on the wall?' Joe says.

'Chipped paint,' says Nathan, 'that's all. That's all.'

He hums a song about bottles on the wall until Joe is quiet, sleeping with open eyes, a drop of whisky drying on his chin. When he wakes, life seems better. Joe wants to talk about other things again. He wants to tell Nathan about the biscuit game, how to make liquor with a tin of pineapple chunks and sun, the tattoos his friends have on body parts that make him laugh till he cries. 'Sometimes bad shit is what makes guys buddies,' he says. 'Bad shit that boys get into together.'

This is the Joe Nathan likes, the one that says the sort of things he thinks he should write down.

'Sometimes, I worry . . . I'm scared . . . ' Nathan says, then he stops.

'Nathaaaan. Nathan? Come down. I need a hand.'

His mother calls him downstairs.

'Tell her nothing if you love her,' Joe says. 'Sometimes silence is the best gift you can give.'

Nathan nods, leaving Joe guarding the ledge, the light fading. Tell nothing, that's just the sort of thing Joe always says. Nathan thinks of this going into the kitchen, where his mother drops pins on the lino. She stretches up on the noses of her bunny feet to tack a *Welcome Home* banner to the wall.

'Pass me the pins, Nathan,' she says.

He passes the pins. Helen sits on the floor, scribbling her name on the cupboard door. The card Mum helped her make lies on the counter, a wax rainbow and stars on the front, night and day all at once.

Nathan holds out his hand to help his mother down from the stool.

'You haven't signed Helen's card,' his mother says. 'Write something lovely.'

She hands him a pen as if knowing he is too big for crayons. Nathan stands at the kitchen counter with the pen. He knows he should write something like *hero* somewhere inside the card and he starts writing it. The *he* starts out fine, then he sees he started too close to the edge. It's trickier to squeeze what comes next into the space that is left on the page.

AUTHOR'S ACKNOWLEDGEMENTS

This book was made possible by Imogen Pelham, thanks to her belief in short stories, by the Costa Short Story Award, and by Stefan Tobler.

I would like to acknowledge the editors and judges who first published some of my stories. I am grateful to Ashley Stokes, *The Pygmy Giant*, Sophie Payle and the Short Story Competition for accepting stories when I started. And to readers and writers who have shared my stories online and supported me over the years. There are too many to name, you know who you are. You kept me writing, particularly Anne Louise Kershaw and her relentless belief, my friend Kate Fox, who brought me a flying pig when I wanted to quit, and the Bristol Prize, with their dedication to the short story.

This book would not exist without my husband, who has never doubted.

It is dedicated to anyone who has felt like giving up, but did not.

Dear readers,

We rely on subscriptions from people like you to tell these other stories – the types of stories most publishers consider too risky to take on.

Our subscribers don't just make the books physically happen. They also help us approach booksellers, because we can demonstrate that our books already have readers and fans. And they give us the security to publish in line with our values, which are collaborative, imaginative and 'shamelessly literary'.

All of our subscribers:

- receive a first-edition copy of each of the books they subscribe to
- are thanked by name at the end of these books
- are warmly invited to contribute to our plans and choice of future books

BECOME A SUBSCRIBER, OR GIVE A SUBSCRIPTION TO A FRIEND

Visit andotherstories.org/subscribe to become part of an alternative approach to publishing.

Subscriptions are:

£20 for two books per year

£35 for four books per year

£50 for six books per year

OTHER WAYS TO GET INVOLVED

If you'd like to know about upcoming events and reading groups (our foreign-language reading groups help us choose books to publish, for example) you can:

- join the mailing list at: andotherstories.org/join-us
- follow us on Twitter: @andothertweets
- join us on Facebook: facebook.com/AndOtherStoriesBooks
- follow our blog: Ampersand

This book was made possible thanks to the support of:

AG Hughes
Adam Butler
Adam Lenson
Adrian May
Aidan Cottrell-Boyce
Ajay Sharma
Alan Cameron
Alan Ramsey
Alannah Hopkin
Alasdair Thomson
Alastair Dickson
Alastair Gillespie
Alec Begley
Alex Martin
Alex Ramsey
Alexander Balk
Alexandra Buchler
Alexandra de
    Verseg-Roesch
Ali Conway
Ali Smith
Alice Nightingale
Alison Bowyer
Alison Hughes
Alison Layland
Allison Graham
Alyse Ceirante
Amanda Dalton
Amanda Jane Stratton
Amanda Love Darragh
Amelia Ashton
Amy Allebone-Salt
Amy Capelin
Andrea Davis
Andrew Lees
Andrew Marston

Andrew McCafferty
Andrew van der
    Vlies
Andrew Whitelegg
Angela Thirlwell
Ann McAllister
Ann Van Dyck
Anna Britten
Anna Demming
Anna Milsom
Anna Vinegrad
Anna-Karin Palm
Annabel Hagg
Annalise Pippard
Anne Carus
Anne Claire Le Reste
Anne Lawler
Anne Maguire
Anne Marie Jackson
Annie McDermott
Anthony Quinn
Antonio de Swift
Antony Pearce
Aoife Boyd
Archie Davies
Arline Dillman
Asher Norris
Averill Buchanan
Ayca Turkoglu

Barbara Adair
Barbara Mellor
Barbara Thanni
Barry Hall
Bartolomiej Tyszka
Belinda Farrell

Ben Schofield
Ben Smith
Ben Thornton
Benjamin Judge
Benjamin Morris
Bianca Jackson
Blanka Stoltz
Bob Richmond-
    Watson
Brenda Scott
Brendan McIntyre
Briallen Hopper
Brigita Ptackova
Bronwen Chan
Bruce Ackers
Bruce & Maggie
    Holmes
Bruce Millar

C Baker
C Mieville
Calum Colley
Candy Says Juju
    Sophie
Caroline Mildenhall
Caroline Perry
Carolyn A Schroeder
Catherine Taylor
Cecilia Rossi
Cecily Maude
Charles Beckett
Charles Fernyhough
Charles Lambert
Charles Rowley
Charlotte Holtam
Charlotte Middleton

Charlotte Murrie &
    Stephen Charles
Charlotte Ryland
Charlotte Whittle
Chris Day
Chris Elcock
Chris Gribble
Chris Hancox
Chris Lintott
Chris Watson
Chris Wood
Christina Baum
Christine Luker
Christopher Allen
Christopher Terry
Ciara Ní Riain
Ciarán Oman
Claire Seymour
Claire Tranah
Clare Keates
Clarissa Botsford
Claudio Guerri
Clifford Posner
Clive Bellingham
Colin Burrow
Collette Eales
Courtney Lilly
Craig Barney

Damien Tuffnell
Dan Pope
Daniel Arnold
Daniel Barley
Daniel Carpenter
Daniel Gillespie
Daniel Hahn
Daniel Hugill
Daniel Lipscombe
Daniel Sheldrake

Daniel Venn
Daniela Steierberg
Dave Lander
David Archer
David Craig Hall
David Gould
David Hebblethwaite
David Hedges
David Jones
David Roberts
David Smith
Dawn Hart
Deborah Bygrave
Deborah Jacob
Deborah Smith
Denise Jones
Diana Brighouse
Diana Fox Carney

E Jarnes
Eddie Dick
Elaine Rassaby
Eleanor Maier
Eliza O'Toole
Elizabeth Bryer
Elizabeth Costello
Elizabeth Draper
Emily Diamand
Emily Jeremiah
Emily Rhodes
Emily Taylor
Emily Williams
Emily Yaewon Lee &
    Gregory Limpens
Emma Bielecki
Emma Kenneally
Emma Teale
Emma Timpany
Eric E Rubeo

Erin Louttit
Eva Tobler-Zumstein
Evgenia Loginova
Ewan Tant

Fawzia Kane
Federay Holmes
Fi McMillan
Finnuala Butler
Fiona Graham
Fiona Malby
Fiona Marquis
Fiona Quinn
Florian Andrews
Floriane Peycelon
Fran Carter
Fran Sanderson
Frances Chapman
Francis Taylor
Francisco Vilhena
Freya Carr
Friederike Knabe

G Thrower
Gabrielle Crockatt
Gavin Collins
Gawain Espley
Genevra Richardson
Geoffrey Cohen
Geoffrey Fletcher
George McCaig
George Sandison &
    Daniela Laterza
George Savona
George Wilkinson
Georgia Panteli
Gill Boag-Munroe
Gillian Jondorf
Gillian Stern

Gina Dark
Glyn Ridgley
Gordon Cameron
Gordon Mackechnie
Grace Dyrness
Graham R Foster
Graham & Steph
  Parslow
Guy Haslam

Hannah Ellis
Hannah Perret
Hanne Larsson
Hannes Heise
Harriet Mossop
Harriet Owles
Helen Asquith
Helen Bailey
Helen Buck
Helen Collins
Helen Weir
Helen Wormald
Helena Taylor
Helene Walters
Henrike Laehnemann
Holly Johnson &
  Pat Merloe

Ian Barnett
Ian McMillan
Inna Carson
Irene Mansfield
Isabella Garment
Isobel Dixon
Isobel Staniland

JP Sanders
Jack Brown
Jacky Oughton

Jacqueline Crooks
Jacqueline Haskell
Jacqueline Lademann
Jacqueline Taylor
Jacquie Goacher
Jade Yap
James Attlee
James Cubbon
James Huddie
James Portlock
James Scudamore
James Tierney
James Upton
James Wilper
Jane Brandon
Jane Watts
Jane Whiteley
Jane Woollard
Janet Mullarney
Janette Ryan
Jason Spencer
Jeff Collins
Jen Grainger
Jen Hamilton-Emery
Jennifer Higgins
Jennifer Hurstfield
Jennifer O'Brien
Jennifer Stobart
Jenny Diski
Jenny Newton
Jeremy Weinstock
Jeremy Wood
Jerry Lynch
Jess Wood
Jessica Kingsley
Jessica Schouela
Jethro Soutar
Jillian Jones
Jim Boucherat

Jo Elvery
Jo Harding
Joanna Ellis
Joanna Neville
Jocelyn English
Joe Robins
Joel Love
Johan Forsell
Johannes Georg Zipp
John Allison
John Conway
John English
John Fisher
John Gent
John Griffiths
John Hodgson
John Kelly
John Nicholson
John Steigerwald
Jon Gower
Jon Lindsay Miles
Jon Riches
Jonathan Evans
Jonathan Watkiss
Joseph Cooney
Joshua Davis
Judy Kendall
Julian Duplain
Julian Lomas
Juliane Jarke
Julie Freeborn
Julie Gibson
Julie Van Pelt
Juliet Swann

KL Ee
Kaarina Hollo
Kapka Kassabova
Karan Deep Singh

Kari Dickson
Karla Fonseca
Katarina Trodden
Kate Beswick
Kate Gardner
Kate Griffin
Kate Young
Katharina Liehr
Katharine Freeman
Katharine Robbins
Katherine El-Salahi
Katherine Jacomb
Kathryn Lewis
Katia Leloutre
Katie Brown
Katie Martin
Keiko Kondo
Keith Alldritt
Keith Dunnett
Kevin Acott
Kevin Brockmeier
Kevin Pino
Kinga Burger
Kristin Djuve
Krystalli Glyniadakis

Lana Selby
Larry Colbeck
Lauren Cerand
Lauren Ellemore
Leanne Bass
Leigh Vorhies
Leonie Schwab
Leri Price
Lesley Lawn
Lesley Watters
Leslie Rose
Linda Dalziel
Lindsay Brammer

Lindsey Ford
Lindsey Stuart
Liz Clifford
Liz Ketch
Liz Tunnicliffe
Liz Wilding
Loretta Platts
Lorna Bleach
Louise Bongiovanni
Louise Rogers
Louise S Smith
Lucia Rotheray
Lucie Donahue
Lucy Caldwell
Luke Healey
Lynda Ross
Lynn Martin

M Manfre
Mac York
Madeleine Kleinwort
Maeve Lambe
Maggie Livesey
Maggie Peel
Maisie & Nick Carter
Malcolm Bourne
Mandy Boles
Marella Oppenheim
Margaret Jull Costa
Maria Pelletta
Marina Castledine
Marina Galanti
Marina Lomunno
Marion Cole
Mark Ainsbury
Mark Howdle
Mark Lumley
Mark Richards
Mark Stevenson

Mark Waters
Martha Gifford
Martha Nicholson
Martin Brampton
Martin Conneely
Martin Hollywood
Martin Price
Martin Whelton
Mary Nash
Mary Wang
Mason Billings
Mathias Énard
Matt Oldfield
Matthew Francis
Matthew Lawrence
Matthew O'Dwyer
Matthew Smith
Matthew Todd
Maureen Freely
Maxime Dargaud-Fons
Michael Harrison
Michael Holtmann
Michael Johnston
Michelle Bailat-Jones
Michelle Roberts
Miles Visman
Milo Waterfield
Mitchell Albert
Monika Olsen
Morgan Lyons
Murali Menon

Nadine El-Hadi
Nan Haberman
Naomi Frisby
Naomi Kruger
Nasser Hashmi
Natalie Smith
Natalie Wardle

Nathan Rostron
Neil Pretty
Nia Emlyn-Jones
Nick Chapman
Nick James
Nick Nelson & Rachel
Eley
Nicola Cowan
Nicola Hart
Nina Alexandersen
Nina Power
Noah Birksted-Breen
Nuala Watt

Octavia Kingsley
Olga Zilberbourg
Owen Booth

PM Goodman
Pamela Ritchie
Pat Crowe
Patricia Appleyard
Patrick Famcombe
Patrick Owen
Paul Bailey
Paul Brand
Paul C Daw
Paul Dettman
Paul Gamble
Paul Hannon
Paul Jones
Paul M Cray
Paul Miller
Paul Myatt
Paula Edwards
Peter Burns
Peter Law
Peter Lawton
Peter McCambridge

Peter Murray
Peter Rowland
Philip Warren
Philippe Royer
Phillip Canning
Piet Van Bockstal
Piotr Kwiecinski
Polly McLean
Pooja Agrawal
PRAH Recordings
Pune

Rachael Williams
Rachel Kennedy
Rachel Lasserson
Rachel Van Riel
Rachel Watkins
Read MAW Books
Rebecca Atkinson
Rebecca Braun
Rebecca Carter
Rebecca Gillam
Rebecca Moss
Rebecca Rosenthal
Richard Ellis
Richard Jackson
Richard Martin
Richard Smith
Rishi Dastidar
Rob Jefferson-Brown
Robert Gillett
Robin Patterson
Robin Woodburn
Rodolfo Barradas
Ros Schwartz
Rose Cole
Rose Oakes
Rose Skelton
Rosemary Rodwell

Rosemary Terry
Rosie Pinhorn
Ross Macpherson
Rossana
Roz Simpson
Rufus Johnstone
Ruth Diver
Ruth F Hunt
Ruth Van Driessche

SJ Bradley
SJ Naudé
Sally Baker
Sam Cunningham
Sam Gordon
Sam Ruddock
Samantha Sawers
Samuel Alexander
Mansfield
Sandra de Monte
Sandra Hall
Sara D'Arcy
Sarah Benson
Sarah Bourne
Sarah Butler
Sarah Salmon
Sarah Salway
Scott Morris
Sean Malone
Sean McGivern
Seini O'Connor
Sergio Gutierrez
Negron
Sharon Evans
Sheridan Marshall
Sherine El-Sayed
Sigrun Hodne
Simon James
Simon John Harvey

Simon Okotie
Simon Pare
Simon Pennington
Simone O'Donovan
Siobhan Higgins
Sioned Puw Rowlands
Sonia McLintock
Sonia Overall
Sophia Wickham
Stefano D'Orilia
Steph Morris
Stephanie Carr
Stephen H Oakey
Stephen Pearsall
Stewart McAbney
Sue & Ed Aldred
Susan Shriver
Susan Tomaselli
Susie Roberson
Suzanne Smith
Sylvie Zannier-Betts

Tammy Harman
Tammy Watchorn
Tamsin Ballard

Tania Hershman
Tasmin Maitland
Thomas JD Gray
Thomas Bell
Thomas Fritz
Tien Do
Tim Jackson
Tim Theroux
Tim Warren
Timothy Harris
Tina Andrews
Tina Rotherham-
    Winqvist
Todd Greenwood
Tom Bowden
Tom Darby
Tom Franklin
Tony Bastow
Tony & Joy Molyneaux
Torna Russell-Hills
Tracy Northup
Trevor Lewis
Trevor Wald
Tristan Burke
Troy Zabel

Val Challen
Vanessa Nolan
Vanessa Jackson
Vasco Dones
Venetia Welby
Victoria Adams
Victoria Walker
Visaly Muthusamy
Viviane D'Souza

Wendy Irvine
Wendy Langridge
Wenna Price
Wendy Toole
Wiebke Schwartz
William G Dennehy

Yukiko Hiranuma

Zara Todd
Zoe Brasier
Zoë Perry

Current & Upcoming Books

Title: *Don't Try This at Home*
Author: Angela Readman
Editor: Stefan Tobler
Copy-editor: Sophie Lewis
Proofreader: Alex Billington
Typesetter: Tetragon, London
Typeface: Swift Neue
Series & Cover Design: Hannah Naughton
Format: Trade paperback with French flaps
Paper: Munken LP Opaque 70/15 FSC
Printer: TJ International Ltd, Padstow, Cornwall, UK